THE LOST LEVEL

THE LOST LEVEL

BRIAN KEENE

An Apex Publications Book
Lexington, Kentucky

This novel is a work of fiction. All the characters and events portrayed in these stories are either fictitious or are used fictitiously.

The Lost Level
ISBN: 978-1-937009-10-6
Copyright © 2015 by Brian Keene
Cover Art © 2012 by Kirsi Salonen
Title Design © 2015 by Geoffrey Blasiman
Typography © 2015 by Maggie Slater

Published by Apex Publications, LLC
PO Box 24323
Lexington, KY 40524

Printed in the United States of America

First Edition

w w w . a p e x b o o k c o m p a n y . c o m

For
Mark and Paula Beauchamp...

ACKNOWLEDGEMENTS

Thanks, first and foremost, to Jason Sizemore and the Apex Books team for their infinite patience and understanding when this project inexcusably went way beyond deadline. Thanks, as well, to Maurice Broaddus for preventing them from killing me. Thanks also to my valiant pre-readers, Mark "Dezm" Sylva, Tod Clark, and Stephen "Macker" McDornell—and also to Bryan Smith and Mary SanGiovanni who acted as additional pre-readers. Thanks to the Apex editorial team: Lesley Conner, Sara Price, and Janet Harriett. Thanks to the cover artist Kirsi Salonen. Thanks, as well, to John LeMay, for lending me his Jeep. Thanks to Cassandra, Kasey Lansdale, and Kelli Owen. Special thanks to Joe R. Lansdale for convincing me to step outside my comfort zone. And as always, more than anyone else, thanks to my sons.

And finally, a note of appreciation and admiration for the works of Edgar Rice Burroughs, Robert E. Howard, Sid and Marty Krofft, Roy Thomas, Joe R. Lansdale (again), Mike Grell, John Eric Holmes, Karl Edward Wagner, Otis Adelbert Kline, Carlton Mellick III, H.G. Wells, and others who inspired this lost world/time travel homage.

1

A TRAVELING MAN

MY NAME IS AARON PACE, and I'm writing this by hand in a spiral-bound, college-ruled notebook that I found in a student's backpack inside of an abandoned school bus. All three—the notebook, the backpack, and the school bus—have seen better days. For that matter, so have I.

The notebook paper is wrinkled and curled, and many of the pages are water stained or smudged with dirt. The backpack is one of those vinyl and canvas kinds you can buy at Wal-Mart, emblazoned with cartoon characters on the back. I don't recognize any of the cartoon characters, but there are a lot of things in this place that I don't recognize, because they're not originally from this world. The backpack is one of those things. I found it attached to a child's skeleton in the back of the bus. It is still in relatively good shape—the backpack, rather than the skeleton—but both shoulder straps have been slashed, rendering it useless and impractical for my purposes. The skeleton is missing its lower half. The hips and pelvis are shattered. I have no way of knowing if that happened before or after the child died, but I suspect it was the former. The bus has some broken windows, four flat tires, and a giant gash in the side where something clawed through the metal to get at the kids inside. There are dried brown smudges splashed all over the vehicle's interior. The splashes could be old dirt, but dirt doesn't usually have a spray pattern. More likely, they're blood.

There is a lot of it, but then again, that's also not uncommon to this place. This is the Lost Level. This is where things become lost. Why should blood be any different?

It's impossible to know how long the bus, the backpack, or the skeleton have been here, because there is no time in the Lost Level. The sun—if that's what it is, and I have strong suspicions that it's not—never changes position in the sky. We live in a perpetual state of high noon. If we have a moon or stars here (or things masquerading as moons and stars) then I've never seen them. The only visible body in the heavens above is that everpresent sun, mocking us with its cruel, unforgiving light. But despite the constant illumination, it is easy to find darkness here. There are deep canyons and a massive, spiraling network of caves and tunnels below ground where the light never reaches, and there are sections of the forests and jungles where the vegetation grows so thick that the sun's rays can't penetrate it. Go look in any of those places, and you will find darkness.

And if you can't find it there, then all you have to do is look inside yourself.

There is a darkness inside of me. I have lost everyone that I care about—from both before I came here, and after. Especially after. They are lost, and I am lost.

Lost here in the darkness of an eternal sunshine.

Lost in the Lost Level.

Anyway, I suppose I should recount how I got here and what has happened to me since then, before this pen goes dry or I run out of paper. Or I get eaten. Or worse. I've given up hope that anyone from back home will ever read this, but it's important to me that I get it down on paper regardless, if only just to prove that I once existed. That I was once alive, and had thoughts and feelings. It would be nice if, after I am gone, others knew my story. Perhaps, one day, someone from my world will stumble across this notebook, and read what I have written here, and I will live again, if only for a little while and if only within these words. And who knows? Maybe that's what passes for an eternal life inside this place. Perhaps that is the best we can hope for in the Lost Level.

I doubt there is enough paper for me to tell you everything. I'd need a dozen notebooks or more for that. But it is my sincere hope that I can at least tell you how I came here and what happened after. That I can tell you about Kasheena and Bloop. If you have just arrived here, some of this information might just save your life.

I'll write as much as I can, until I run out of room. Which, when you think about it, is how life goes. Our story continues until there are no pages left to write it on.

So...my story. I was born and raised in Byron, Minnesota. My father was a Methodist minister and my mother worked from home part-time as a court stenographer. Every day, they'd send her audio recordings of court cases, and she would transcribe them. It seemed like boring work, but I never heard her complain. I had two siblings—an older brother and a younger sister. We were never wealthy, but our parents made sure we never wanted for anything, either. In short, I had a good, safe, middle-class upbringing. We lived in a parsonage next to the church, who paid for the home, thus freeing my parents of the responsibility of a mortgage.

As a kid, I read a lot of comic books and paperback novels. Sometimes I wonder if people back home still do. Read paperback novels, that is. Right before I came here, there was a lot of talk about electronic books. I doubt something like that would ever truly replace printed books, but I can't be sure. Some of the things I've found here can only have come from a future timeline, and given that they are far enough advanced that I can't figure them out, reading a book on a computer doesn't seem so far-fetched anymore.

Anyway, I was a voracious reader. I especially enjoyed sword and sorcery tales and loved reenacting them in the woods behind the church. Using sticks or plastic swords, I fought mock battles with my brother and our friends. In high school, I took up fencing. I also joined a Historical Reenactment Society and worked summers at the local Renaissance Fair. Both activities allowed me to hone my sword-fighting skills even more. When not doing that, I dabbled in Live Action Role-Playing games with my friends. Not only was I proficient with a sword, I also became pretty good with firearms, thanks to the father of a friend of mine who used to take us target shooting and deer hunting each year. Tramping around the Minnesota wilderness in winter will toughen up any kid. I was a deadly shot with a rifle, bringing down my first buck—a six pointer—when I was twelve. With a pistol, from a distance of seventy-five yards, I could put a grouping of six shots close enough together to fit a half-dollar over them. Eventually, I earned varsity letters for football and wrestling, as well.

I hope you don't get the wrong impression. I wasn't a jock by any means. If anything, I was considered an oddity by my fellow teammates because of my interest in things like reading and the fact that, in addition to my athletic ability, I studied and applied myself and got good grades. Indeed, my books granted me educational opportunities that my otherwise middle-class upbringing could have never afforded.

Something else I discovered in high school was a rabid interest in occultism and religions other than Christianity. Maybe this was my own form of teenage rebellion against my father, although if so, I wasn't consciously aware of it. I loved my father. I respected him and the rest of my family, as well. But all the same, I didn't share my family's beliefs. When I sat there in church on Sunday and listened to my father's sermons, I didn't feel anything. In truth, I would venture that a portion of the rest of the congregation didn't feel anything either. That had nothing to do with my father's skills as an orator. He was passionate and emotive and always tried to make things interesting. Overall, he was an excellent speaker. Despite this, I sometimes glanced around and saw old men sleeping, women balancing their checkbooks or fanning themselves with church programs and staring off into space with dazed expressions, and small children playing with cars or dolls beneath the pews. It eventually dawned on me that these people were not there every Sunday because they believed, or because they enjoyed listening to my father speak. They were there only because it was what they were expected to do. They were expected to attend church services every Sunday. For them, it had become habit. Routine. The church lacked energy. It lacked spirit. That bothered me. I wanted to feel that universal spirit I'd heard so much about. I wanted to be filled with it. And if I couldn't find it with God, I reasoned, then perhaps I would have better luck finding it elsewhere.

A trip to the local mall provided me with a start. I went inside the bookstore there and found the occult and metaphysical section, which was comprised of exactly two shelves sandwiched between Bibles and Western novels. I'd already read my father's Bible and my grandfather's complete (if somewhat battered) collection of Zane Grey and Louis L'Amour westerns. What I wanted was in that small middle section.

That first visit to the 'New Age' section introduced me to the Simon paperback version of the dreaded *Necronomicon*. I was familiar with the book from my readings, but too young to know that the Simon edition was a fake. Attracted by the lurid cover and the book's reputation, I bought it and read it. Hell, I devoured that book. It was like a switch had been clicked on inside of me (sadly, it wasn't until years later that I beheld the real *Necronomicon*). I returned to the bookstore every week after that, and soon I'd discovered everything from Crowley's *Magic in Theory and Practice* to Lavey's *The Satanic Bible* to various paperbacks on Wicca and other pagan religions. After reading everything my local bookstore had to offer, I started perusing the free occult texts that were available online.

By the time I earned a full scholarship and entered college, I'd worked my way through most of the readily available occult tomes and now spent my weekends haunting antiquarian bookstores, looking for the rarer, esoteric volumes. And that was how I first discovered the Labyrinth.

I could fill up the rest of this notebook writing about the Labyrinth, and still not explain it fully. Since I don't have the time or capability to do that, I will have to give you the CliffsNotes version. If you have a layman's grasp of string theory, or if you've ever read a Marvel or DC comic book, or watched an episode of *Doctor Who* or *Star Trek*, then you'll understand the basics of the Labyrinth. Provided they have those things where you come from, of course. Not every place does, as I've learned from some of my fellow castaways over the years.

The Labyrinth is perhaps best described as a dimensional shortcut through space and time. It touches and connects everything. Most of humanity remains ignorant of its presence, but it is explored and utilized by madmen, magi, occultists, and a few in the highest levels of world government. The only times the rest of humanity sees the Labyrinth is when we die, dream, have an out-of-body experience, or alter our consciousness in some manner, perhaps while under the influence of certain perception-enhancing substances. It is not actually a labyrinth, but that is how mankind has perceived it over the millennia, and thus, that is how it has gotten its name.

Imagine the universe. Picture our galaxy and all of the other galaxies beyond ours, both known and unknown, that make up the universe. Then consider all of the planets in each of those galaxies. The Labyrinth connects to all of them, and by utilizing it, one can travel from planet to planet and galaxy to galaxy. But it goes far beyond that. Interplanetary travel is just the beginning. Our planet, our galaxy, and our universe have different versions of themselves that exist in other dimensional spaces. Some people call these alternate realities. Devotees of the Labyrinth refer to these alternate dimensions as levels. As one occult tome explained it, *"Just as there are different planets in the sky, there are also different versions of those planets, existing simultaneously on a different level of the universe. Beings, including humans, can traverse this multiverse of levels by means of The Labyrinth."*

By using occult methods, one could access the Labyrinth and through it, visit an Earth just like the one I came from, or maybe one where the Germans won World War II, or where North Korea launched a nuclear war in the year 2008, or where dinosaurs never became extinct and continued to evolve instead. And just as you could travel to alternate Earths, so could you explore the alternate realities of other planets—a Mars filled with lush vegetation or intelligent life, if you liked, or a Mercury cool enough to walk on. All of these levels were accessible to a practitioner who had the knowledge and will to do it. And I resolved that I would be such a practitioner.

The one thing I came across time and time again in my studies was the mention of a "Lost Level"—a dimensional reality that existed apart from all the others, a place where the flotsam and jetsam of space and time occasionally washed up from across the shores of the multiverse. It was supposedly a place where one could encounter creatures and beings and objects from, quite literally, anywhere in the multiverse. All mentions of the Lost Level warned that while it could be accessed by a traveler, there was no escape from it. The Labyrinth led into it, but there was no exit, except in death—and even then, the scholars seemed divided. Some said souls and spirits could escape the Lost Level. Others said those energies remained trapped within it. Regardless, the one thing I've learned since my arrival here is that no one gets out of the Lost Level alive.

I wish now that I had heeded those warnings, but I was young and headstrong and stupid. I have matter from the entire universe beneath my feet, and yet I am homeless.

Accessing the Labyrinth—finding a door, opening it, and traversing the dimensions—was a long and complicated process, and again, I'll have to be brief in my explanations of it. During a careful study of ley line maps, I found a place of power at a lake about one hundred and twenty miles southwest of Duluth and decided to begin my experiments there, as such places were traditionally favorable for rituals such as this. On my first attempt, I went there in the afternoon, chose a remote location far removed from prying eyes, and set up my tent. I'd fasted all day, and I was lightheaded with hunger and a strange mix of fear and excitement. It was hard to stay focused, but I did my best. I felt ready. Pure. Having a healthy body, mind, and spirit is important in magick, as is possessing a sense of self-assuredness and confidence. The key to success is making the universe revolve around you—understanding that you are the focal point of all that occurs.

I crawled inside the tent and meditated for a while. When it was time for the ritual to begin, I grabbed my backpack and went outside. Using the compass and GPS feature on my phone, I found north and faced in that direction, making sure there were no tree limbs or other obstructions directly over my head. Satisfied with my choice of location, I found a stick and used it to scratch a circle into the forest floor, at a depth of about a quarter inch—just enough to clear the dead leaves and disturb the soil. Then, I filled that circle with salt. Returning the salt canister to my backpack, I pulled out a red blanket and spread it out on the ground inside the circle, making sure none of the fabric overlapped the circle's edges. Then, I placed four red candles in four different positions—north, south, east, and west. I lit each of them and then retrieved a small incense burner from my backpack. I filled it with a tiny amount of scented oil and lit that, too. When it was burning, I reached into my pocket and pulled out a piece of paper on which I had drawn the required symbols for this particular ritual. I touched one end of the paper to the flame and let the ashes fall into the oil, holding it there even as my thumb and index finger burned. I winced, clenching my teeth and resolving to feel no pain. When the paper had been consumed, I sat down cross-legged in front of the incense burner and faced north again. Finally, with my left hand, I pulled out my final item—a pocketknife my father had given me for my tenth birthday—and sliced the ball of my right thumb.

"I have fasted according to the Nomos," I said. "The Nomos is the Law. I have eaten nothing unclean. I have drunk only water. I have avoided spilling my seed and have abstained from worshipping at the temples of Ishtar or Lilith. Thus, I have kept my essence and remained pure. My candles are of the appropriate and required color and were lit at the appropriate time. With them, I cast light upon the four Gates of the Earth, even as I face the Northern Gate. There is no roof over my head, except for the sky. I have done these things in accordance with the Nomos, which is the Law, and thus, I command your attention."

I held my bleeding thumb over the burning oil and squeezed out three drops of blood. As I did this, I repeated the incantation three times. "Ia unay vobism Huitzilopochtli. Ia dom tergo Hathor."

Finished, I paused for a moment, sucking at the cut. The taste of my own blood made me feel queasy, but I shrugged that sensation off. I pressed the wound against my jeans and waited for it to stop bleeding. When it did, I continued.

"I sit in the appropriate and required manner, and am safe inside my circle of protection. You cannot harm me. I come here with respect to open a gate. I come seeking passage. And so, I call upon the Gatekeeper, who gave to us the Nomos, which is the Law. I call upon the Doorman, who is the Burning Bush and the Hand That Writes and the Watchman and the Sleepwalker. I call upon he who is named Huitzilopochtli and Ahtu. He who is named Nephrit-ansa and Sopdu. He who is named Hathor and Nyarlathotep. I call upon him whose real name is Amun. And thus, by naming you and offering my blood three times, I command an opening."

Nothing happened. I held my breath, waiting. My heart beat once. Twice. Three times. Then, the oil began to smoke. Wisps curled from the incense burner and rose into the air. The smoke seemed to be meeting resistance from something, even though there was nothing there. The wind was still. There wasn't even the faintest hint of a breeze. I glanced down at my thumb, and when I looked up again, a doorway floated in front of me, hovering just a few inches from the ground. On both sides of the doorway was my world, but inside the door was another level. Through it, I glimpsed a scene very similar to the one I stood in—a forested lakeside after dark. Steeling myself, I stepped through into that other world. Sure enough, it was an almost exact duplicate of my own level, except for one telling difference. When I looked up at that other reality's sky, the constellations were very different than my own. Indeed, they were different than anything I had ever seen from my Earth. Most telling was a long, crooked scar running across the face of the moon, a shadow that had no counterpart on my own moon.

I only stayed on the other level for a few minutes that first time, and when I emerged back through the doorway into my world, I was scared and shaken and didn't sleep for two days. I had no appetite and ended up struggling with an unexpected and deep melancholy. But that didn't stop me from trying again. If anything, it just encouraged me. The depression passed, and my hunger returned—and with it, a thirst for more.

On my second attempt, the doorway opened into another alternate reality. This time, I found myself looking at a city. At first, I wasn't sure which one. They have always looked alike to me, especially American cities, where the architecture is usually the same, and the streets are filled with chain stores, fast food restaurants, and discount outlets. The doorway hovered directly over a busy sidewalk, and people bustled around the portal without even giving it a glance. I assumed that only I could see it. I stepped through the door and explored the city a little—half a block, no more, endeavoring to keep the doorway within my sight at all times. I found a newspaper at a bus stop and skimmed through it and found out that I was in Chicago. This level was much like our level and dealt with the same problems—global recession, terrorism, a new arms race, social unrest, the politics of polarization, and a media that focused more on entertainment news and celebrities rather than issues of actual importance. But there were subtle differences, as well. The President of the United States was somebody named Anthony Genova. On this level, Microsoft was the manufacturer of the iPod and iPhone. And the Chinese had launched a successful return to the moon in the year 2000. This act had since been followed by landing human beings on Mars, beating Russia and the European Federation there by a projection of five years, even as the American space program was discontinued due to a lack of funds.

I stayed in that world for an hour, never straying far from the door. I determined that this alternate America's cash was the same as ours and bought something to eat from a sidewalk vendor. I watched some television in a storefront window and listened to music booming from car speakers as the traffic crept by. I didn't recognize the television program or the various snatches of songs. When I returned through the doorway, I brought the newspaper with me as a souvenir. I wasn't sure I would be able to, and when I closed the doorway and stopped the spell by extinguishing the oil, I half expected the paper to vanish, but it didn't. It was still there, proof that I really had traveled to an alternate reality. When I got home, I hid it safely.

This time, upon my return, I felt none of the adverse side effects I'd experienced the first time. Instead, I felt excited and euphoric. Rather than becoming depressed, I was simply impatient to do it again as soon as possible.

So, I did.

My excursions grew more frequent—and more daring. I never did master the art of opening the door on a specific location. Instead, my attempts were similar to channel surfing. But I did become adept enough that I no longer needed to work the ritual from a place of power. I began doing them from the comfort of home, rather than the woods, opening doors into the Labyrinth and visiting other levels from the rooftop of my apartment complex in the dead of night when everyone else was asleep and I wouldn't be spotted. I visited a world where the Nazis controlled America, and one where the gas crunch of the late-Seventies had turned us into a Third World economy from which we'd never recovered. I went to other time periods in our level's history—the Old West, the Sixties, and what I think was a time about fifty years in my future. I can't be sure about the latter because I spent all of my time there hiding in an alley as a series of massive explosions rocked the city I was in.

I also glimpsed other worlds, realms, and dimensions completely different than Earth. Out of an abundance of caution, I never set foot in any of them, although the desire to do so was strong. The first one I saw was a desert planet, coated with red sand, much like we are told the conditions on Mars are like (although I have my doubts about that). A human skeleton lay there in front of the door, dry and desiccated. Nothing else moved in that wasteland except a group of scarlet dust funnels, dancing lazily in unseen wind currents. I didn't like the funnels. They reminded me of mini-tornadoes, and I had the uneasy impression that they were alive. I can't explain why I came to that conclusion, but I felt it strongly. Suspecting the air there was poisonous, I stepped back from the door, lest any fumes cross over from that level to mine. Another time, I glimpsed a world populated by what I think were robots, but nothing lived there, either—at least nothing constructed of flesh and blood and other organic material. The last alien level I saw was a city composed entirely of crystal. It, too, was empty and lifeless, and so utterly alien in architecture and dimensions that I grew uneasy just gazing upon it. After watching it for too long, my stomach turned nauseous and my vision grew blurry.

That wasn't how I felt when I first gazed upon the Lost Level, though. You must remember that I didn't know that's what it was upon that initial encounter. When I first saw it, I was transfixed by the beauty and splendor of a lush, green, tropical jungle. I saw palm fronds and ferns gently bobbing in the wind, and a white-tailed deer with velvet-coated antlers nibbling at some low-hanging leaves. Mistaking the dimension for an alternate reality of my Earth, I stepped through the doorway. In doing so, I startled the deer, who ran away. The ground was soft beneath my feet, a mixture of white sand and soil. The air was warm and humid, but a cool breeze caressed my scalp through my crew cut. I sighed, then smiled.

"This is paradise," I murmured. "Maybe I'll stay here awhile."

A buzzing insect hovered around my ear. I slapped at it and then turned back to the door.

But the doorway was gone.

At first, I was too shocked At first, I was At first, too shocked I was At first, I shocked At first, I was too shocked too shocked At first, too shocked I was too At first, At first, I was shocked shocked too shocked I was too shocked At first, I was At first, I too I was shocked At first, shocked At first, I was too shocked I was I was too shocked too shocked At first, I was too shocked At first, shocked At first, I shocked At first, I was too shocked At first, I was too shocked I was At first, I shocked At first, I was too shocked too shocked At first, too shocked I was too At first, At first, I was shocked shocked too shocked I was too shocked At first, I was At first, I too I was shocked

2.

BLADES
OF GRASS

AT FIRST, I WAS TOO shocked to do much more than stare. I was certainly too surprised to even think about being scared. I turned around, and blinked, but when I looked again, the door was still gone. Stunned, I ran back to the spot where it had been and put my hands out, feeling for it, but they passed through the air and met no resistance. The door hadn't just closed. If that had been the case, I would have still been able to see it there, or at the very least feel it. No, this was something far worse. The door through the Labyrinth—and my only way back home—had vanished.

Only then did the fear set in. I'm ashamed to say that I whimpered like a lost puppy. My frightened sobs grew louder and more frantic, with no concern for who or what might hear me, until I finally began to rave like a madman. I just kept repeating "No" over and over again, so fast that the words just sort of blended together. It sounded more like "Nuhnuhnuh" than anything intelligible, and had anyone saw me, they would have thought me insane. Perhaps I was. I certainly felt so at that moment; crazed with terror at the prospect of being trapped on another world or dimension—whichever it was, I didn't know, but neither possibility appealed to me. In desperation, I tried the invocation again, but without the proper accoutrements, the ritual was useless. I ended up on my knees, clawing at the dirt and crying out, but the door didn't return. The Labyrinth was sealed off, and with it, my way back home.

Eventually, I gathered my wits. More buzzing insects darted around my eyes and ears, their tiny drones bringing me back to my senses. I slapped at one as it landed on my neck and felt it squish across my palm. I glanced down at my hand and frowned. The crushed insect looked much like a mosquito, but its blood was bright green, the color of a lima bean, and it smelled slightly alkaline. Wrinkling my nose, I wiped my hand on a nearby leaf.

Moments later, my palm began to tingle and then burn. When I looked at it, the skin was red and swelling. The pain quickly grew intense, like a bee sting, but much stronger. Tiny welts popped up on my skin, like the blisters caused by poison ivy. I stripped off my t-shirt and wiped away the rest of the noxious fluid as best I could. Then, swatting the shirt back and forth to keep the insects away (just as a cow or a horse does with its tail) I began to make my way through the jungle. My hand throbbed. There was a small game trail cutting through the foliage. I guessed that it had been made by the deer I'd seen earlier, or perhaps a herd of similar animals. If so, then there was a good possibility that the trail would eventually lead to some sort of water source, so I decided to follow it.

Before doing so, I noted my surroundings so that I could find this spot again. If I could obtain the ingredients needed to effect another opening ritual, it might be possible to regain entrance to the Labyrinth and find my way home. That was what I told myself at the time. Of course, I know better now.

I am lost, and I can never go back. This is my home now, for better or worse.

I started along the trail, and other than swatting at the persistent bugs, I did my best to be quiet and stealthy. My pulse hammered in my chest, and my body tingled with nervous tension. Fortunately, the pain in my hand had slowly begun to subside. The flesh was still red and puffy, but already the swelling was starting to go down, and the blisters had receded. Whatever the poison inside the mosquito was, my allergic reaction to it had been mild.

Trying to remain calm, I trudged along the narrow footpath. The sun hung overhead, its bright rays occasionally breaking through the thick, leafy canopy overhead. I mentioned earlier that the sun here never changes position and that we live in a perpetual state of high noon. I didn't notice this until later on that first day, but as I climbed the trail up a hill where the trees thinned and eventually cleared, I did get the uncanny impression that this dimension's sun was much closer to this world than my own sun, and that it was smaller, as well.

"Where am I?" My voice was hoarse after all the crying I'd done. "Where the hell is this place?"

A glint caught my eye, the sunlight flashing off something in the dirt at my feet. I knelt down and found a silvery coin half buried in the footpath. I dug it out with my fingers and brushed it off, examining it. The coin looked just like an American quarter from my world, complete with George Washington on the front and an eagle emblazoned on the back. The date stamped on it was 1958. I paused, wondering what this find meant. Was it possible that I was in another alternate reality version of my world and just hadn't discovered civilization yet? Or was it more likely that another traveler from my world had dropped the coin here on this level? Both were possibilities. Ultimately, the only way to tell was to continue onward and keep exploring. I stuck the quarter in my pocket and looked around.

The game trail wound down the hillside and back into the dense jungle again. I took note of a few large rocks jutting from the dirt. They looked banally normal—the same type of rocks I could find in the yard back home in Minnesota. The vegetation around me was the same, as well. Granted, there were no lush jungles in Minnesota, but the ferns, palm trees, vines, and other plants all looked very Earth-like. The strange mosquitoes had disappeared, perhaps in search of a meal that didn't swat back. I could almost convince myself that I was indeed back home on my level. I closed my eyes for a moment and let the breeze blow over me. It felt good on my sweaty forehead and chest. I stood there and listened to the sounds around me. Insects buzzed and chirped in the greenery, and I heard a number of birdsongs. None of them sounded particularly alien.

Now that my panic had subsided, and the pain in my hand had completely disappeared, I began for the first time to logically consider my predicament. While I still thought it was a good idea to follow the footpath and find water, I decided to inventory my pockets and figure out exactly what I had with me. As it turned out, I didn't have much. I always traveled light when journeying through the Labyrinth. I'd left my wallet, phone, and keys back home in my apartment. All I had on me was a wad of bills, a few coins (including the one I had just dug out of the dirt), and my jeans, underwear, socks, and boots. My shirt made a fine fly swatter, but I was hesitant to put it back on again. The venom had left ugly discolored stains on it, and just in case the poison was still potent even when dry, I didn't want to wear the shirt for fear it might seep into my skin from the fabric. I had no desire to experience that pain again, no matter how briefly.

It occurred to me that perhaps I should search for the things I'd need to re-open the doorway from this side, but I had no idea where I'd find salt, a red blanket, red candles, or oil in this world. All of these were required ingredients for the ritual. There were other ways of accessing the Labyrinth, true, but I'd neglected to study them after having so much initial luck with this method. Only then did I realize the inherent foolishness in such a single-minded pursuit of study. I'd grown overconfident and cocky, and now that self-assuredness had left me stranded.

Sweat ran into my eyes, stinging them. Sighing, I wiped my brow and then got to my feet again. I returned the money to my pocket. I thought of my parents, and my brother and sister, and my few friends. The distress they would suffer, not knowing what had happened to me—the thought was crippling. For a moment, I felt another surge of panic, but I fought it down, certain that if I succumbed to it now, I would die right there on that hilltop. I wasn't ready to give up or die. I wanted to get back home. Strengthening my resolve to do just that, I started down the trail again.

When I reached the bottom of the hill, I found myself once more surrounded by thick vegetation. The insect and bird sounds stopped, and the jungle became still. I wondered if it was my presence that had caused this silence, or if there was some sort of predator about. I walked slowly, creeping along, trying to stay alert. I found a stick that was as long as me and about an inch thick. Testing it, I found the wood to be sturdy and sound. It would make a fine walking staff, and though I doubted I could do much with it as far as a means of self-defense, it made me feel more confident to hold it.

Armed with my new staff, I came to a spot where the trail was overgrown with a snarl of vines. Strange leaves sprouted from them. Their shape and sheen reminded me of poison ivy, but they were pink in color, turning to a deep magenta at the tips, and they gave off a noticeably sweet scent that reminded me of honeysuckle. A few butterflies flitted around them, the same size as the butterflies back home, but with multi-colored wing patterns of blue, purple, orange, and green. They seemed to be feeding on the leaves. I'd always been under the impression that butterflies ate shit—literally, based on how many of them I'd seen alighting on the marshy area of the grass above our septic tank when I was a kid—but these particular butterflies were apparently attracted to the sweet aroma coming from the vines. Despite that, the similarity of the leaves to poison ivy made me wary. Rather than just shoving my way through, I pushed the foliage aside with one end of my stick. There was no immediate reaction from the plant. I'd half expected the leaves to eat through my staff with some type of corrosive sap. The butterflies scattered, alarmed by my intrusion, and I paused, considering them for a moment. The foliage, insects, and placement of the sun certainly seemed to indicate that this level was not an alternate version of Earth, but then how to explain the American coin I'd found? And if this wasn't an Earth, then where was I? It seemed like the more I tried to figure it out, the more confused and frustrated I became. I decided instead to focus again on more immediate things like finding food and water and shelter.

After clearing the path, I continued on my way. Soon, I became aware of the sound of trickling water. I slowed my pace even more, listening carefully. The sound got clearer. Pushing through some ferns, I paused. Twenty yards ahead, a deer stood with its back to me. Its head was bowed, and it lapped from a small spring trickling from an outcropping of moss-covered rock alongside the trail. I wasn't sure if it was the same deer I'd seen earlier, but it certainly looked identical, right down to the fuzzy velvet on its antlers. I stood there, watching in silence as it drank, overwhelmed with its simple beauty and majesty. Then, the wind shifted and the deer caught my scent. Its white tail twitched. It raised its head, saw me, and snorted. Its eyes widened in fear. Then it darted off, running down the path and disappearing into the foliage. Even after it had vanished from sight, I heard it rustling through the undergrowth. Soon, the sound faded.

I approached the spring. The water looked clean and inviting. I decided that if the deer was drinking it, then it was probably safe for me to do the same. If there were parasites or other dangers in the water, I'd rather face them than die of thirst. I cupped my hands under the trickle and filled my palms. Then I rubbed my hands together, washing the remaining remnants of bug venom from them. Satisfied that my hands were clean, I then drank. The water was crisp and cold and pure, tasting just like bottled spring water back home. I gulped it eagerly, filling my cupped hands again and again until my thirst was sated. Then I splashed water on my face and neck, washing the sweat away and relishing the coolness against my skin. Reinvigorated, I smiled, forgetting all about my situation for a moment. Finally, I decided to try cleaning the venom out of my shirt.

I had just stuck my shirt under the trickling water and was rubbing the fabric briskly when I heard the deer cry out in pain. There was no mistaking the sound. I'd heard deer back home make the same noise when a hunter's misplaced bullet or arrow didn't kill them right away. As I stood there listening, the poor creature cried out again. There were no other noises—no growls or sounds of struggle to indicate that it had been attacked by a predator. I wondered if perhaps the deer had tripped or fallen in its rush to flee from me. If so, and it was disabled or injured, then it was my duty to put the poor thing out of its misery. I couldn't stand the thought of an animal suffering, unless perhaps it was a snake. I've always loathed snakes, even non-poisonous ones, and usually killed them on sight.

The deer squealed again. Forgetting about cleaning my shirt, I tied it around my waist. Then I grabbed my walking stick and rushed down the trail. After a few dozen yards, I emerged into a wide clearing that was free of trees or overhead growth. Sunlight filled the area, illuminating a bizarre and horrific scene. Large swaths of green grass grew on both sides of the trail. The deer lay on its side in the middle of the grass, bleeding profusely from dozens of cuts and gashes. Something had slashed it from head to tail. When I saw what it was, I gasped.

The injured animal thrashed, trying to escape, and the grass swayed, slicing at the deer. Each individual blade of grass was like a razor blade, and they moved in tandem, cutting through fur and flesh. Blood gushed out over the blades and into the dirt, vanishing as quickly as it spilled, slurped up by a thirsty network of roots beneath the soil. The deer shuddered and screamed as the grass rustled and writhed, slashing its abdomen open with a frightening, savage precision and delivering a mortal wound. The animal's eyes rolled up white in its head. Warm innards splashed out onto the ground. Despite the temperature of the day, steam rose from the pile of offal. The blades of grass began dicing the organs into smaller bits, while more blood was sucked into the dirt.

My heart went out to the deer, but there was nothing I could do for it. There was no way for me to reach it without stepping onto the grass myself, not even with my staff. And besides, the poor animal was already dying. Its movements had slowed to spasmodic twitches. Taking a deep breath, I ran down the trail, making sure I avoided stepping into the grass on either side. Somehow, the grass knew I was there. The blades moved, slashing at my ankles, but they weren't long enough to reach me. I shuddered at the thought of what they could do to me should I make one misstep.

Clearing the patch, I plunged back into the jungle again, following the footpath. For a while, I viewed all of the vegetation around me with fear and suspicion. Every tree, every leaf, every vine, branch, twig, and flower became a cause for alarm. I recognized some of the plants. Others were utterly alien to me. I passed through a wet, marshy area covered in yellow mushrooms that quivered and swayed at my approach—so I went around them. In another area, I heard leaves whisper overhead. When I glanced up at the tree branches directly above me, I noticed the limbs moving despite the lack of a breeze. I hurried past, expecting a claw-like branch to descend and snag my arm at any moment. The leaves grew silent as I moved on.

Eventually, the ground began to rise again, and the foliage grew less thick. Jungle vegetation gave way to sparsely forested hillsides and boulders. The game trail ended at a narrow, shallow gorge. I stood at the edge, peering down. The bottom of the gorge was strewn with rocks, and the bones of an animal skeleton lay scattered and broken among them. The bones belonged to something I couldn't identify. The body was like that of a large cat, perhaps a panther or a tiger, but the skull was similar to a wooly mammoth's, and it had three eye sockets instead of two. One glance at the skeleton's tusks and claws convinced me that I didn't want to meet a living specimen out here while I was unprotected and defenseless, so I continued on my way, going around the gorge and hiking up into the hills. My staff thudded dully against the rocks.

As I walked, I wondered what new terror awaited me next. In a world where even something as seemingly innocuous as a blade of grass could kill you, what hope did I have?

3

CAVE AND CACHE

I DON'T KNOW HOW LONG I walked, but eventually, I found the Jeep.

I was scaling up a treacherous outcropping of rock and having second thoughts about it. When I'd started the climb, I hadn't thought the going would be so difficult. My original intent had been to reach a high vantage point and survey the land around me. I was especially interested in any signs of intelligent life—smoke from a campfire, or perhaps huts or a village or maybe even a city. Instead, all I saw were more trees. The forest and jungle (because they seemed to grow amongst each other at points) ran all the way to each horizon. When I finally spotted a thin, curling line of white smoke, I wasn't sure what it was at first. I thought perhaps it was a cloud or fog. It was drifting up from the trees. When I realized that it was indeed smoke, I decided to climb higher in the hopes of seeing the source.

My progress became even more grueling. Unlike the jungle below, there was no footpath cutting through the boulders and ridges, and the rocks grew steeper and sharper the higher I went. Reluctantly, I had to give up my walking stick, since I needed both hands to climb. I cast it aside with some regret. That simple stick had given me courage and focus and a sense of protection. I watched the staff clatter off a boulder far below, snapping in half as it plunged from sight. Then, I returned to my arduous climb. I looked carefully before each hand-hold or footstep, mindful of snakes. Given what I'd seen from the mosquitoes and grass of this world, I could only imagine what the serpents might be like. The very idea terrified me.

Although it looked barren, this region was just as alive as the jungle had been. Birds circled overhead, their shadows painting the rocks. Spiders, ants, centipedes, and other insects skittered in the crevices. Some of them looked normal. Others were strangely colored. A tiny brown lizard, the size of my thumb, poked its head out at me from a crack in the rocks and then vanished. A bird squawked overhead. It sounded like a crow, but was much smaller.

Occasionally, the slight breeze turned into a quick gust of wind that whistled through the ravines and peaks. The sun remained where it was, seemingly frozen at high noon. Sweat dripped from my hair, nose, and upper lip, and ran down my back and shoulders.

I glanced below again, but the smoke I'd spotted earlier was now gone. Sighing with frustration, I decided to keep climbing anyway, in the hopes of spying it again and ascertaining its source. Smoke most likely meant one of two things—either a wildfire or a campfire. Judging by the shape of the column I'd seen, I judged it had been the latter, and that was a good thing. A campfire meant some other form of intelligent life. So, I continued my climb.

I was about fifty feet from the peak, clinging to a jagged, triangular outcropping of grey, lichen-covered stone which teetered above a steep, almost vertical drop to more rocks far below, when I spotted the Jeep. It was painted red, with big, fat tires, a roll cage, and a black canvas top attached to the roll bars. The front half of the vehicle was sticking out of a cliff face to my right. The rear of the Jeep wasn't visible. Indeed, it was fused with the rock, as if the vehicle had materialized on the hillside, half in and half out of the cliff.

Overcoming my initial surprise, I edged my way over to the precariously suspended vehicle and managed to get the driver's side door open. The hinges squeaked and flakes of rust drifted down into the gorge below. I clambered inside and sat down. Sure enough, the bucket seats gave way to sheer cliff face. It felt like I was sitting inside some bizarre sculpture, as if someone had carved an incredibly realistic vehicle out of granite. But when I reached out and touched the Jeep, I felt steel and vinyl, rather than rock. I was nervous at first, half-expecting the cab to snap off and plummet into the ravine, but it didn't. It didn't even wobble as I moved around. It was truly fused with the stone behind it, becoming just another outcropping in the cliff face.

I sat there for a moment, wondering how this was possible and what it meant. That was my first inkling that I was in the fabled Lost Level that I'd read about—that dimension from which there is no exit, where cosmic castaways wash up and are abandoned. Several occult tomes had suggested that doorways to this dimension could sometimes open at random, without magical means. It had been proposed that this was the secret behind everything from the Bermuda Triangle to some of the thousands of missing persons cases each year. Could that have been what happened here? Maybe a temporary doorway had opened up back home (or in a reality similar to my home) and this Jeep had driven through it, materializing here, high above the jungle. And then the doorway had closed just as abruptly, leaving the vehicle half-embedded in solid rock. But if so, where was the driver?

My hands were scraped and chafed from crawling up the rocks, and my jeans were torn and dirty. I'd lost my shirt somewhere along the way, too. I'd had it tied around my waist when I started climbing, but now it was gone. Despite the heat, I started shivering.

"Shock," I muttered. My voice sounded strange to my own ears. "You're going into shock. You need to focus, Aaron. You've had a very stressful day, so focus on the tasks at hand."

I did just that, starting with a thorough search of the Jeep's interior. It had obviously been there a while. In addition to the rusty door hinges, time and exposure to the elements had faded the seat covers and left the vinyl dashboard cracked and dirty. The windshield was covered with a thick coat of dirt and dead bugs. Most of the insects appeared normal, except for one that was as big as my fist and looked like a cross between a bumblebee and a caterpillar. A key-ring filled with keys dangled from the ignition. The floor was filthy, and the scattered remains of a bird's nest poked out of the cup holder. I tried the glove compartment. It was unlocked. Inside was a green plastic folder containing the vehicle registration and insurance information. The Jeep belonged to a John LeMay of Statesboro, Georgia, and the vehicle registration card had expired in October of

2001. I wondered if somewhere back in Statesboro, Mr. John LeMay was listed as a missing person. I put the folder aside and continued rooting through the glove compartment. There was a pile of faded, crinkled paperwork, half a pack of chewing gum which had long since hardened, and a tube of lip balm. I pulled the cap off the lip balm and smelled it. There was a hint of cherries. I rubbed some on my lips and found that it was okay. I stuck the tube in my jeans pocket and kept searching. The cherry flavor made my mouth water. Worse, it made me strangely homesick.

My fingers brushed against something hard and metallic hidden beneath the papers. I grabbed the object, pulled it out, and whistled with appreciation. It was a .45 handgun, weathered and in desperate need of a cleaning, but still perfectly functional. I released the magazine and checked it. There were a total of eight bullets in the magazine, plus one more inside the chamber of the gun. I ejected that one into my palm and studied it. Mr. John LeMay had apparently reloaded his own ammunition, judging by the flattened lead flush with the edge of the brass casing. I chambered the round again and engaged the safety.

"Thank you, John LeMay, wherever you are."

Encouraged by this find, my trembling subsided, and I felt a burst of renewed energy. I was in a bad spot, certainly, but I would persevere. I sat the gun next to me on the seat and kept searching.

There was an empty plastic bag on the floor. I grabbed the paperwork from the glove compartment and stuffed the pile inside the bag, thinking it might come in handy later if I needed to start a fire. Unfortunately, the Jeep's owner hadn't been a smoker. There were no matches or lighters to be found. In the center console compartment, I discovered several compact discs. I added them to the bag. I could snap the plastic and fashion it into arrowheads or spear tips, and the discs' reflective backsides might prove useful if I needed a mirror. Also in the console compartment were a cell phone charger and adapter, a small pair of collapsible binoculars, a ballpoint pen, and broken pair of sunglasses. The binoculars were a great find, and I grabbed them right away. I added the charger and adapter to my bag, thinking I could use the cords for something—as makeshift fishing line perhaps. I also took the pen. Beneath the driver's seat was a dirty travel mug. Something rust-colored had dried inside of it, but I dropped it into the bag, as well. I assumed the stain was just coffee or tea, rather than blood.

On a whim, I reached for the key ring. There were about a half-dozen keys on it. They jangled as my hand brushed against them. I pumped the gas pedal and then turned the key, but the Jeep didn't start. It wasn't until I'd tried it a third time that I realized the gas tank was located in the part of the vehicle that had been fused with the rock. Did that half of the Jeep even exist anymore? Had its atoms joined with the cliff face? Or was the rear half of John LeMay's Jeep still back in Georgia? I turned the key back to the accessory position, wondering if the Jeep's battery still worked. I tried the headlights, but they were dead. Experimenting with the stereo produced similar results. Sighing, I pulled the key from the ignition and put the key ring in my pocket, thinking I might be able to fashion the keys into tools or weapons at some point.

My stomach grumbled. I was still tired and hungry, but I felt a little better about my situation now that I was armed with something more than a walking stick. Once I'd found food and shelter, and had a chance to rest, I intended to start looking for a way back home. I considered retracing my steps and turning to the jungle to find the corpse of the deer, but the thought of trying to free the dead animal from the razor-grass seemed foolish. I'd have better luck hunting something I didn't have to fight another predator for—especially if that predator was a plant that could slice me to ribbons. A .45 is a formidable handgun, capable of stopping almost any attacker—from an armed intruder to a bear in the wild—but it wouldn't do much against blades of grass. I'd be better armed with a weed whacker or a lawnmower.

After tying the plastic bag's handles around one of my belt loops, I stuck the .45 in my waistband. The metal felt cool against the small of my sweaty back. I'd made sure no rounds were chambered and wasn't too worried that I'd accidentally shoot myself while climbing down. I clambered out of the Jeep and out onto the rocks, scaling the cliff face like a spider. I descended at a different point from my initial climb, and in doing so, I noticed something I hadn't seen before. On the other side of the peak lay a long, shadowed crevice. A narrow, winding trail snaked along the bottom of it, providing less treacherous footing and more importantly, an escape from the ever present sun.

I eased around the cliff face, working my fingers into the cracks, and lowered myself onto a jumble of boulders just above the crevice. I glanced at the jungle and forest far below, admiring once again the strange, crazy-quilt geography of this strange dimension. There was no sign of the smoke I had spotted earlier. Instead, it had been replaced with a shimmering heat haze that seemed to blur everything. The trees looked so small from this height. I was reminded of the tiny replicas that had come with the model train set my father had set up in the basement for my siblings and me when we were kids. At that moment, I felt older than I was, and the distance between where I now was and my family still were seemed like an unimaginable gulf.

I clambered down from the boulders and, with some relief, stood on solid ground again. I was about to enter the crevice when I startled a bird that had been nesting between the rocks. It resembled a chicken, but it was smaller, and its feathers were light grey. It moved faster than any hen or rooster I'd ever seen. The bird squawked with fright as it flew away. Startled, I steadied myself against a boulder while my pulse resumed its normal pace. I found the nest after a quick search, but there were no eggs in the tangle of sticks and grass. My stomach rumbled again.

I pulled the binoculars out of the bag and tried to track the bird. I scanned from the left to the right, but couldn't find it in my field of vision. I was just about to give up when I caught sight of something glinting in the sun, far, far away at the base of the hills. I focused the binoculars, zooming in on the location, and what I saw made my breath catch in my throat.

Five figures marched toward the jungle. Each of them was similar to a man, having two arms, two legs, and a head, but that was where the likeness stopped. Instead of being human, they were reptilian in nature. Their greenish-grey skin was covered with scales, and they had serpent's heads, complete with fangs and flickering tongues. They had three fingers and a thumb on each hand and stood an average of seven feet tall. Their weight and shape varied, but overall they seemed to be slender and wiry. They carried a variety of weapons—everything from crude swords and crossbows to rifles of a sort like I'd never seen. They also wore a strange assortment of armor and gear. One was dressed in what appeared to be police riot armor, complete with a mirrored-visor helmet that didn't quite fit over its snake-like head. A second wore some type of chainmail garb. A third was dressed in what looked like the very old and rusted armor of a Roman centurion. The other two wore leather armor with strange patchwork. I squinted, blinking the sweat from my eyes, and tried to focus the binoculars better. Gasping, I felt my gorge rise. The leather was human skin. The patchwork was faces and tattoos and in one case some type of surgery scar.

I'd felt an instant sense of loathing upon first spying the serpent men, for as I mentioned before, I've always had an unnatural and deep-seated hatred of snakes. That emotion turned to anger and revulsion upon seeing the flayed human skin that they'd so callously draped themselves in. My first impulse was to pull out the .45 and open fire, but I resisted. They were too far away, and the weapon was essentially useless at that range. The old adage came to mind—a handgun is only useful for defense until you can make it back to the rifle you should have been carrying with you in the first place. Instead of shooting them, I continued to watch, unable to look away no matter how much I wanted to. They moved in tandem and seemed to be communicating with one another, although no visible speech or hand movements were apparent.

Suddenly, the leader stopped. Behind him, the others did the same. As one, they slowly turned in my direction, staring directly up at me. I knew that I was too far away to be seen, hidden as I was behind the rocks, but I still ducked down in fright. Had it just been coincidence, or had they really known I was there, and if so, how? My scent? That seemed unlikely, given the distance between us. Telepathy, perhaps? Some sort of sixth sense? Or maybe it was just bad luck. Maybe they weren't looking at me, or perhaps they had heard the bird I'd spooked. I crouched there with my back against the stones until my breathing and heart rate had returned to normal. Then, I carefully raised the binoculars and peeked over the edge again. The snake men were farther away now, moving into the jungle. Sighing with relief, I wiped the sweat from my brow and returned my attention to the shadowed crevice.

Dirt and gravel crunched beneath my boots. I went slow, watching for scorpions, spiders, or anything else that might be lurking among the cracks. I came across an animal skeleton. The bones were yellowed and moldy and scattered so badly that it was impossible for me to identify what they had belonged to. I also spotted some rabbit tracks in the dirt. How was it that something so familiar—something like a rabbit, or a Jeep, or the quarter I had found—existed simultaneously with snake men, and razor-grass, and three-eyed tigers with wooly mammoth tusks?

My thoughts returned to the serpent men. In my occult studies, I'd read of a supposed race of ancient amphibians known as the Dark Ones, who were said to have resided on Earth at one time, and indeed, as some speculated, still lived in cities beneath the ocean, far from the prying eyes of mankind. They were a highly intelligent race, able to fashion tools and weaponry and harness beasts of burden and possessed arcane knowledge. But by all accounts, the Dark Ones were said to look more like Gila monsters or Komodo dragons. The Reptili-ans I'd witnessed earlier were decidedly snake-like. Could they have been a distant cousin of the Dark Ones? An evolutionary offshoot, perhaps? Or were they something entirely different? Perhaps even alien?

As I continued my exploration, the winding crevice grew nar-rower, and the rock walls loomed far overhead. Moss and lichen covered the stones in a blanket of green, brown, grey, and hues unlike any I'd seen before—orange and red and yellow. I avoided touching any of them. It was cooler here in the shade, and for that I was grateful. The sun had me perplexed at this point. I was certain that it hadn't moved in the whole time I'd been on this level, and because of that, I had absolutely no sense of direction or time. All I knew was that I was exhausted from my ordeal, and famished, and needed to rest soon before I collapsed. So, when the crevice eventually ended at the mouth of a narrow cavern, I felt a mix of gratitude and apprehension.

I approached the opening with caution. It was a narrow sliver about eight feet high and four feet wide, and it sloped steeply down into the hill. I couldn't see very far into the darkness, but a cool breeze drifted out of the cave, and the air smelled okay. Sticks, rocks, dead leaves, and other detritus lined the floor. I stood there listening, but heard nothing inside save the faint sound of dripping water.

Slowly, I stepped through the opening and followed the slope downward. While the cavern mouth had been narrow, it opened up considerably once I was inside. The walls stretched a good fifteen feet across, and the corners and space ahead of me were shrouded in darkness. The air grew noticeably cold after only a few feet inside. The floor was damp and muddy in some places, and I had to choose my steps carefully to avoid slipping. The cave leveled off after about forty feet, and I was able to stand without sliding. I waited for a bit, letting my eyes adjust to the gloom, but even then, I couldn't see very far. I wished I had the means to start a fire, but I had no matches or a lighter, no flint or steel, and had never been able to master the friction technique even though I'd spent several camping sessions attempting it by rubbing sticks together when I was a kid. I considered returning to the Jeep and trying the battery again. If I could get a spark off of the terminals, I might be able to catch the spark in something combustible, and then fashion a torch and carry it back here. But after considering the items I had in inventory, I didn't think that would be possible, especially given the fact that I doubted the battery had a spark left in it. And I wasn't sure I'd be able to make the climb while clutching a flaming torch in one hand.

When I decided my vision wasn't going to adjust any more than it already had, I explored the cave. Arms outstretched, I slowly walked into the shadows on one side and felt my way around. There was a sheer drop off near the back, nearly hidden in the darkness, which made my asshole pucker and my testicles tighten and shrink as I stood at the edge. Had I not waited until my eyes adjusted before I'd gone exploring, I would have certainly fallen in it. I had no way of telling how wide or deep the chasm was, but it *felt* immense. Draughts of cold, dank air drifted up from it, and the sound of dripping water was more prominent. I knelt, selected a stone, and dropped it into the darkness. Although I crouched there listening for a very long time, I did not hear it strike anything. I tossed another stone beyond the hole, trying to determine how far across it stretched. Again, I heard nothing.

Taking a deep breath, I backed away from the edge of the pit and continued my explorations. I'd almost reached the far side of the cavern when my foot struck something on the floor. Whatever it was, it made a dry, rattling sound, followed by a metallic clank. Panicked, I stumbled over something that felt like a stick and heard more objects scattering under my feet. I knelt again and felt around. It wasn't until I found the skull that I realized what it was I'd tripped over—a skeleton. It was human, judging by the feel, and must have been there for quite some time given how easily it fell apart when my foot struck it. There were a few scraps of musty fabric attached to some of the bones and some moldering splinters of moss-covered wood lying amidst the bones. I wasn't sure what the wood had originally been part of, but it was useless for my purposes now. My fingers sank into it and came away damp and musty. Remembering the metallic sound, I felt around some more until my fingers fell across a cold length of steel. I ran them down the shaft until I found a hilt. I couldn't believe my luck! It was a sword. I wondered about its owner. Who had they been? Were they even human? I considered carrying the bones back into the light and examining them, but decided I was too exhausted.

Regaining my bearings, I carried the sword back to the entrance of the cave, where the light was better. I examined it with appreciation. Sunlight glinted off the blade. It was a beautifully crafted weapon, of a style and design I was unfamiliar with. Despite the fact that I'd found it lying in a damp cave, there wasn't a spot of rust on it. The blade was still razor sharp, and free of dings or notches. I tested it out, checking its weight and balance, and was amazed. Never had I held such a weapon. It was absolutely perfect. Whoever had made it, they'd been a true craftsman. My spirits soared once more. I forgot all about being trapped in another dimension. Possessing such a weapon as this would make my stay here much easier, no matter how long the duration.

Satisfied with my find, I set about making camp. The cavern entrance was narrow enough that I could easily defend it should the snake men return. Obviously, the rear of the cave was dangerous only if I sleepwalked, which, to the best of my knowledge, I had never done before and had no plans of doing now. I laid out my gear, keeping the handgun and the sword within easy reach, and wished for food and water. Tomorrow, I'd have to start the day with a concerted effort to find both, and that meant returning to the lowlands. My head ached, and my jaw felt tight. Both were signs of dehydration and hunger. They would only get worse if I didn't do something soon. I sorted through my loose change and stuck a nickel in my mouth. I had read somewhere that if you sucked on a coin, it worked up saliva in your mouth and eased a thirst. In reality, all it did was make my mouth taste metallic and greasy. I spat the coin into my palm, grimacing. My stomach grumbled again.

To take my mind off my hunger, I crouched down at the cave mouth for a while and watched the sun. I don't know how long I stayed there. An hour, perhaps. Maybe more. I do know that it was long enough for my feet to cramp and my legs to go numb, but I stayed as I was, just watching. In all that time, the sun never moved. It remained as motionless as I was. I was certain that it occupied the exact same position in the sky that it had when I'd first arrived here. Something else I noticed was that unlike the sun on Earth, I could stare directly into this sun, and it didn't hurt my eyes. Oh, the glare was still intense, and if I stared too long, I saw funny shapes and blobs in my vision, but it wasn't blinding like the sun back home.

Eventually, the pain in my legs became too much to ignore, overpowering even the cramps in my empty stomach. Groaning, I stood up and stretched. My muscles were so numb that I almost fell over, but the tingling subsided after a bit. I debated trying to meditate, something I'd learned to do in my occult studies, but decided against it. Yawning, I pulled the sword and handgun close and lay down. Using a rock for my pillow, I waited for night to come. It never did, but I slept anyway.

4

BREAKFAST WITH
THE REPTILIANS

I HAVE NO IDEA HOW long I slept that first sun-filled "night." All I know is that I woke feeling unrested, sore, and afraid. My exposed skin was covered with bug bites, my back and neck muscles ached, and my head throbbed—both from having a stone for a pillow and from hunger and thirst. I vaguely remembered thrashing and turning in my sleep, unable to get comfortable. No matter what position I'd lain in, rocks and debris had dug into my skin. Worse, I kept waking up with no idea of where I was. The irony of that fact was not lost on me.

I stretched for a while, trying to work out the kinks in my muscles. When that didn't help, I meditated. Sadly, that was just as futile. I found it impossible to clear my mind and calm my inner self, which is the key to successful meditation. Instead, I found myself thinking back over all of the occult lore and spells I'd learned and was somewhat stunned to discover that I knew nothing helpful. Oh, I could create a circle of protection to guard me from an evil spirit, or I could bind a low-level demon, perhaps, but so far, I hadn't encountered the need for either of those skills here in this strange place. It was frustrating. Why had I never learned how to dowse for water or how to create fire via magical means? Those would have been far more useful given my current predicament. Instead, I would have to rely on my wilderness survival knowledge and my skills with swords and firearms. I doubted a magical circle of protection would help against the snake men I'd seen the day before.

Although I didn't feel the urge, I decided to relieve myself. I went outside of the cave to do my business, on the off-chance that I might have to sleep there again should a better shelter not prove viable, and I didn't want it reeking of piss. I stood next to a boulder and unzipped my fly. My kidneys throbbed and my stream was weak—more evidence of dehydration. Resolving to find food and water before anything else, I collected my few belongings and started back down the treacherous hills.

The first difficulty I encountered was freeing up my hands to climb. The pistol was safely ensconced in my waistband again, resting against the small of my back, but the sword proved more difficult and unwieldy. Finally, I fashioned a makeshift sling out of the cell phone charger wires and cables I'd salvaged from the Jeep, tying one end around the hilt and blade of the sword, and then looping the middle around my neck. The weight wasn't enough to choke me, and it freed up my hands. The only drawback was the steel sword bouncing against my back and shoulders with each step that I took. That quickly became annoying. I had tied the plastic bag to my belt loops again, and it rustled as I climbed. Although game had been scarce in the rocky hills, save for the bird, lizard, and a few insects, that noise would scare away any potential food once I was back amongst the trees. Worse, the bag was starting to get holes in it. I would have to find another means of carrying my gear soon before the plastic tore to the point of uselessness.

I made it back down to the lowlands without incident, but the physical exertion left me winded and dizzy. I paused to rest in the shade of a particularly large palm tree, but the weakness in my limbs didn't abate. Despite a careful search, I couldn't find the trail I'd taken the day before. Cursing, I untied my sword and used it to hack at the curtain of vegetation. Insects swarmed me, buzzing in my face. My progress was slow.

As I slashed through a particularly thick tangle of vines, several of them wrapped around the blade and tried tugging it from my grasp. They were insistent, and their strength surprised me. Gritting my teeth, I wrenched the sword free and attacked, slicing the vines into ribbons. They withdrew, dripping greenish sap. The severed tendrils wriggled and curled on the ground, oozing into the dirt. I prodded one with the tip of my sword. It curled weakly around the blade, but was easy enough to dislodge. They twitched for a few moments, and then lay still.

It occurred to me how utterly alone I was in this place. I'd never been an extrovert, but I'd had a few friends and a loving, caring family, and I missed them now. Worse, I just missed people in general. Back home, it had been nothing for me to go a few days without speaking on the phone or emailing someone, especially when I was involved in my studies. The difference was, had I been lonely back home, I could have reached out to someone. Here, I had no such option. Unless I wanted to initiate contact with the snake men, or conjure up the ghost of John LeMay, I was alone. The realization left me feeling gutted and helpless, and my overall despair deepened. I longed for someone to talk to, even if the conversation was only about trivial things—sports scores or politics or the latest celebrity gossip. I'd abhorred such topics in the past, but they would have been a comfort to me at that moment, because they would have been familiar, and therefore, reminders of home. I'd never felt so far away from everyone and everything I held dear as I did at that moment, and although there have been times since then when I've felt just as lonely, it was never deeper than it was that morning.

Coming across a massive, moss-covered log, I probed it experimentally with the tip of my blade. The wood was soft and the sword sank into it easily. Kneeling, I dug into the log with my fingers. Moist wood disintegrated under my touch. I uncovered white grubs, black and red ants, and other insects. I had no way of knowing whether any of them were poisonous or not, but at that point, fueled by hunger and desperation, I didn't really care. I decided to try the grubs, rather than the ants, as there was less chance of a reaction, based on what I knew of their biology back home. I snatched a plump, wiggling grub from the wood pulp and popped it into my mouth. After a moment's pause, I chewed. The worm exploded inside my mouth, popping like an overripe cherry tomato. Grimacing at the taste—something akin to sawdust and sushi mixed with motor oil—I waited to see if there were any side effects. Other than the foul taste, there didn't seem to be, so I ate the rest of the grubs, albeit slowly. I waited a few moments, but other than the urge to vomit from the nauseating taste, there didn't seem to be any side-effects. Satisfied that I wouldn't get ill, I then continued on my way.

The jungle came alive around me. The trees and bushes echoed with the chorus of a multitude of insects and birds. Some sounded identical to ones that I'd heard all of my life. Others were entirely alien to me. Their cries reminded me again of how alone I was in this place. I considered shooting a few birds, but I was reluctant to waste my limited supply of ammunition, and most of them were small enough that by the time I field-dressed them, there wouldn't be more than a mouthful—if the .45 left even that much behind. Feeling helpless, I plodded on, pushing through the undergrowth, and I swear it sounded like the birds were laughing at me.

At one point, a noise like thunder rumbled overhead. It seemed to go on for a long time, yet when I looked up at the sky, it was still clear and cloudless. I considered the possibility that it was an earthquake or an explosion, but saw no signs of either. The ground wasn't shaking and the trees weren't swaying, nor did I see any disturbances around me. Perhaps more telling, the sound didn't seem to disturb the wildlife. After a few minutes, the roaring faded.

A little while later, I discovered a patch of what looked like watermelons growing wild across the jungle floor. They were of the same size as the ones back home and had the same green and white rind, but I remained suspicious. I wrapped my knuckles on one and found it solid. More so, it sounded ripe. Cautious, I cut the melon open with my sword. It was pink and red on the inside, and the black, teardrop-shaped seeds were certainly familiar. Most convincing was the smell. My mouth watered at the prospect, and so, I tried one. My first tentative taste confirmed that they were indeed watermelons. How they'd come to be here on this level I had no idea, nor did I very much care at that point. I grunted and sighed happily as I gorged myself on an entire melon, gnawing it down to the white of the rind, enjoying a taste of home. My stomach cramped a few times, but I kept it all down. I sliced open a second melon and devoured it at a more leisurely pace. When I was finished, my fingers and face were sticky with watermelon juice, my stomach was full, and my thirst had been slaked. Even better, I could no longer taste the grubs I'd eaten earlier. The sugary fruit had banished the taste from my mouth.

Satisfied that I wouldn't starve to death for a while, I decided to find or build a shelter close to this known source of food. While the cave had suited my purposes the night before, I didn't savor the thought of having to trek back and forth every day for nourishment. Intending to explore the immediate vicinity a bit more, I notched the bark of a few trees with my sword so that I could find the location again, and then I untied my plastic bag of belongings and hid it safely inside a hollowed out stump. Then, armed with only the sword, handgun, and my binoculars, I ventured farther into the jungle in a pattern of concentric circles. I marked several more trees as my search widened, ensuring I wouldn't get lost. I saw a few other fruits, but none of them were as easily identifiable as the watermelons had been. Growing on several trees was something that looked like a cross between a pineapple and a carrot. A few birds pecked at them, so I assumed they were safe to eat. All of the strange, tubular fruits grew high up in the branches, far out of my reach. Tying the sword behind my back again, I shimmied up the nearest tree to pick one and try it.

Doing so saved my life.

I was just about to pull the nearest fruit free of its branch when I smelled something odd. The odor reminded me of cucumbers mixed with moth balls. As a boy, that same peculiar musk had always accompanied the appearance of copperheads, black racers, and other snakes, and I had always known to steer clear of an area when I smelled it. Just like it had in my youth, the smell filled me with dread.

As the stench grew stronger, I noticed a group of ferns swaying back and forth down below. I clung to the tree, trying to remain still, as the ferns parted and a group of figures plunged into the watermelon patch. It was the same group of serpent men I'd spotted the day before. I knew this because they wore the same mismatched armor and carried the same variety of weapons as the group I'd previously spied upon—swords, crossbows, and those strange rifles like something out of a science fiction movie. This close, the flayed human leather armor was particularly horrific. The dried, stretched faces looked as if they were screaming. I was close enough to even make out one of the tattoos on the tanned skin—a cartoonish, Big Daddy Roth-style four-wheel drive truck with four demonic looking characters behind the wheel.

The snake men had an additional member of their species with them, also dressed in leather armor and equipped with an olive-colored canvas backpack. They also had three captives in tow. I suspected that perhaps the four new additions had been left behind at a campsite the day before, which would explain why I hadn't seen them. All three prisoners had their hands bound at the wrists and behind their backs with some sort of durable vine. The same had been done to their ankles, giving them only enough slack to walk with a shuffling sort of gait. Each captive was flanked by two of the creatures. All three captives were naked. The first was a human male, approximately my height, but a lot older than me and much thinner. That's not to say he was skinny. He wasn't. He just lacked any discernable body fat. His chest, abdomen, arms, and legs were lean and sinewy and corded with muscles. His brown hair fell to his shoulders and was peppered with silver strands. His long beard had the same coloration.

The second captive was a male, but I knew that only from his rather prominent genitalia. His penis and the fact that he was bipedal was where all similarities with a human being ended. For starters, he was covered in thick, blackish-blue fur, the texture and length of which resembled a shag carpet. The captive had pointed, cat-like ears and bright yellow eyes. Both his fingers and toes were tipped with black talons, several of which were broken, as if from recent conflict. Most incredible was his long, prehensile tail—a hairless, grey appendage half as thick as his arm, that reminded me of a worm. The serpent men had wrapped the tail around the unfortunate creature's body and tied it with more vines, which led me to wonder if the prisoner could use it as a weapon. Despite being bound, the tail moved and twitched, straining to be free. One of the captors noticed the movement and angrily prodded the furry creature with the tip of its sword. The captive stumbled and tensed, flashing whitish-yellow fangs behind black lips. Then, it continued on. As they passed under my tree, I saw the creature's nostrils flare. For a moment, its eyes flicked upward, but it gave no sign to its reptilian tormentors that it had caught my scent or seen me concealed in the branches.

Then the third captive stumbled into view, and I nearly tumbled out of the tree when I saw her. To say she was beautiful just wouldn't do her justice. I'd heard the term breathtaking before, and until that moment, I had always dismissed it as a literary device. But when I saw her limping along between her captors, my breath literally stopped in my chest. Her luxuriant chestnut and auburn colored hair spilled around her shoulders and curled just above her full, ample breasts. Her skin was bronzed. At first, I thought it was a tan, but after a moment, I realized it was her pigmentation. The sunlight glistened off her flat stomach and the tiny beads of perspiration that dotted the thatch of soft-looking pubic hair between her golden thighs. Her legs and armpits were unshaven, something I'd never seen on the women back home. It was shocking, but also strangely alluring. Compelling, in an exotic, primal sort of fashion. When I saw her eyes, my breath hitched in my chest a second time. The irises of both her eyes were two colors—green and blue. The colors were separated by her dark pupils.

I was awestruck, still admiring her beauty when the snake men stopped simultaneously. They hadn't spoken, or made a sound, but it was clear that they were obeying some unheard signal. One by one, they turned their heads upward, staring at me. Forked tongues flickered from their mouths, and their lips pulled back in snarls, revealing jagged fangs. I couldn't figure out how they'd known I was there, but at that moment, it didn't matter. The two armed with rifles hurriedly unslung their weapons, while two others fell back a few steps and readied their crossbows. I had only seconds to act.

Shouting in a desperate attempt to disorient them, I dropped from the branch and landed atop the shoulders of my closest opponent, crushing the beast to the ground. My sword slapped against my back as he buckled beneath me, and I heard the snake man's bones snap sharply beneath his leather armor. His blood soaked into my jeans and the air filled with its musky tang. The rifle slipped from his scaly grasp. His chest rose once, but his breathing was labored and blood poured from his nostrils and slit-like ears. His eyes narrowed and grew cloudy. Then his breathing ceased. His forked tongue lolled from his mouth. I pulled my pistol, flicked the safety off, and crouched atop the bloody ruin of my opponent, facing off against the remaining five monsters. The hate in their eyes was an almost palpable thing.

But so was their fear.

Looking back on it now, what unnerved me most about that battle was the disconcerting silence in which it took place. The snake men hissed and grunted, but not once did they speak or cry out. I had no doubt they were communicating, but I wasn't sure how they were doing it. They used no spoken words, and made no gestures or other visible signals, yet they moved and fought as a team, seemingly well aware of what their kin were doing during the battle.

Had it not been for the element of surprise and the chaos that my entrance had created, I'm certain they would have surely killed me. As it was, I pressed the attack, taking advantage of their confusion. I acted purely on some savage instinct, driven on by adrenaline and a primal revulsion of my reptilian foes. I snapped the pistol up and fired a shot at a snake man dressed in old, rusted Roman centurion armor. He was in the process of leveling a rifle at me when I shot him. I didn't recognize his weapon. My bullet ripped into his throat, exposed above the breastplate. Blood and scales splattered against the tree trunk behind him, and he toppled backward. A soundless blast erupted from the barrel of the rifle, and the air grew wavy and distorted, like a shimmering heat mirage. I felt a rush of warmth race past me, and the hair on my right arm singed and burned. Then the creature collapsed, dropping the rifle beside him.

I wheeled around, narrowly avoiding the thrust of a sword, and leapt to my feet. Three Reptilians closed ranks around me, trying to hem me in. One was armed with a sword. The second was equipped with a crossbow. The third carried a crude but effective-looking spear whose tip was crusty with dried, brown blood. Their eyes were wide and unblinking. Still gripping my pistol, I drew my sword with my free hand and stood my ground.

"Come on," I challenged. My voice quaked with fear and panic, and I cringed at the sound.

If the creatures understood me, they gave no sign. Instead, they approached slowly, making their way with deliberate caution, trying to force me backward. I knew we were too tightly clustered for the opponent with the crossbow to use his weapon effectively, so the sword and spear were a more immediate concern. I saw movement out of the corner of my eye and wondered where the fourth snake man had gotten to. A second later, there were the sounds of a struggle behind me, and my three opponents charged. I fired two shots at the center mass of the one who was armed with a sword. He wore police riot armor, which stopped the rounds from penetrating, but the force of the impacts knocked him backward. He kept his grip on his sword, but the mirrored-visor helmet flew off his head and rolled across the jungle floor. I side-stepped a thrust from the spear and quickly parried a strike from the third foe, who had dropped his crossbow and now wielded a sword, as well. Our weapons clanged as they crashed together, and the vibrations ran through my arm and up to my shoulder, rattling my teeth.

Behind me, a gunshot rang out and the female captive screamed. I tried to turn around and see what was happening, but the two snake men pressed me, attacking at the same time. The one to my left thrust at my ribs with his spear, while the one to my right swung the sword downward, trying to cleave my arm from my shoulder. I dropped my weapons in the mud and seized the spear with both hands. Then I yanked hard on the shaft and spun the Reptilian around. The sword blow crashed down upon his head, cleaving his skull in two and showering me with gore. I blinked blood and brains from my vision. While the swordsman struggled to free the wedged blade, I ripped the spear from the dead foe's scaly hands and shoved the jagged point into the swordsman's left eye. I didn't stop until it protruded from the back of his head. Instead of falling, he stood there jittering. The snake man's foul-smelling blood slicked the spear's shaft, and then my hands, but I barely noticed.

Turning to face my final opponent, I found that the captives had already taken care of him. A quick glance at the situation told me the story. This snake man, armed with a handgun, had attempted to shoot me in the back, but the older male captive had stopped him. In the struggle, the Reptilian had shot my savior. Then, the third captive—the furry one with the long tail—had intervened. That same prehensile tail was now wrapped around the murderer's throat, choking the life from him. The forked tongue protruded from the creature's lips as it went still. Then, slowly, the furry captive unwound his tail and stared at me with something akin to respect. Slowly, he nodded in recognition.

I returned the gesture and said, "Thanks. I owe you one."

The furry captive grunted in response.

"He does not speak our language," the woman said, and her voice was as beautiful as the rest of her. "But he is a friend."

"No doubt," I replied, nudging the Reptilian with my toe and making sure it was dead. The creature didn't move. I looked up at my furry benefactor, who made a fist and then pounded his chest once.

"Bloop," he declared.

"Nice to meet you, Bloop. I'm Aaron. Aaron Pace." Returning the gesture, I made a fist and pounded on my chest, repeating my name. Then I turned my attention back to the woman. "And what is your name?"

"I am Kasheena. My guardian," she motioned at the dead man on the ground, "was called Kasham. He was my uncle."

I wondered about this. Kasham's skin color did not have the same bronze hue of Kasheena's. Perhaps he'd been her adoptive uncle, or maybe uncle meant something different among her people.

"I'm sorry for your loss," I said.

"Do not be."

"Oh...you weren't close?"

"We were very close, and I loved him much. But I do not weep for him."

I frowned. "Why not?"

"Why would I? He died as all members of our tribe wish to die—defending those we love. There is no greater honor, Aaron Aaron Pace."

"Just Aaron," I corrected her, feeling stupid. My eyes kept focusing on her breasts. I hated the compulsion and struggled against it, but I just couldn't help it. They were impossible not to admire. My face felt flushed, and I stared instead at the ground. It occurred to me that I was covered in snake blood and bits of gore. My hands felt unpleasantly sticky, and the smell was revolting. If Kasheena noticed, she said nothing. The silence seemed to hang there between us, and I struggled for something to say. Finally, I asked her, "So, how did you and Bloop meet?"

"The Anunnaki captured Kasham and I. Bloop was already their captive when we encountered them. I do not know if he has other people here in the land. I have never seen his kind before, nor had my uncle."

"What did they want with you?"

She shrugged, and the things that simple gesture did to her body were absolutely intoxicating. "I am not sure. They have captured others from my tribe before, but none have ever returned. We have sent out warriors to find their lair, but it remains hidden. Some of my people suspect the Anunnaki live deep below the ground. Some say they capture us for breeding. Others say it is for slave labor or food."

"Breeding." I scowled. "That's sick...."

"I do not know what our fate would have been had you not rescued us from the Anunnaki, but I know that I would have chosen death before I would lay with one of their kind. To even imagine such a thing...."

She trailed off, shuddering, and crossed her arms protectively over her breasts.

"Anunnaki," I repeated. "That's what these snake men are called?"

"That is what my people call them. I do not know what they call themselves, for they have never told us. I doubt they speak our language."

"They didn't seem to speak at all."

"Oh, they have a language, but it is not verbal. They communicate with one another via their thoughts."

I was intrigued. "Telepathy? I had suspected that was a possibility before."

"I do not know that word." Kasheena frowned. "Your accent and mode of dress are strange, but we speak the same language. You were not born here in the land. You are from elsewhere."

"Yes, I'm from Minnesota. Have you heard of it?"

She shook her head.

I was quiet for a moment, thinking back on my paranormal studies. While I stood there in thought, she examined her uncle's body, while Bloop swatted at flies with his tail.

"Where I come from," I told her, "the Anunnaki were ancient Sumerian gods. Some people believed they might have been reptilian aliens from the Alpha Draconis star system that visited our planet. Do your people believe the same thing?"

"If it has ever been discussed at length among my people, then I have not heard. But the Anunnaki must indeed have come from elsewhere, just as others here do. And just as you have. It has been said that no creature is original to this land."

"What is this place?" I asked. "Does this land have a name?"

"Shameal says it is called the Lost Level."

I must have been visibly startled, because her eyes widened, and she stepped toward me.

"I see by your reaction that you have heard of Shameal. Have his powers become so legendary that they are known on the other worlds?"

"No. I mean, I've never heard of this Shameal. Who is he?"

"He is our tribe's wise man. A great healer and a mystic. Perhaps the greatest. He knows the ways of this land better than anyone."

"And he calls this land the Lost Level?"

"Yes."

"Is he...can he help me?"

Kasheena cocked her head. "Help you how?"

Bloop grunted and scratched his stomach. Then he swatted with annoyance at a fly.

"Could he help me get back to my world? What you called elsewhere?"

"I do not know," Kasheena said. "I have never known anyone to return to elsewhere. Indeed, I have not known many people from elsewhere. Most of my life, I have lived among my tribe."

"But you said that your tribe believes everyone in this land came from elsewhere."

"Yes, that is what we believe. Originally, our people—and all the other tribes and creatures who live here—came from some-where else. My ancestors did. My uncle did, as well, when he was just an infant. But I was born here."

"And no one has ever left this place, as far as you know?"

"Of course people leave. There are some who have left the tribe. They have ventured out into the land to make their own way. And then there are those who died. They have also left, of course. When we die, we leave here."

"But has anyone ever returned to...elsewhere?"

"I do not know. This is a question for Shameal. If you will help me return safely to my people, I will take you to him. He will answer your questions. I am sure of it."

"Why is that?"

"Because my father is the leader of our tribe. He will be happy to see me return, and he will wish to thank you for safeguarding me. If Shameal will not assist you, then my father will order him to do so. As great as Shameal is, my father is greater. Shameal respects him, as do all."

"And how far away is your village?" I asked.

"If we rest normally, then it is five sleep's journey."

"Five sleeps..." It occurred to me that with a perpetual sun, the inhabitants of this land had no way to mark the passage of time via days and nights—at least no way that I would recognize.

"Five sleeps," she repeated. "If we were to travel through the swamp, the journey would be much shorter, but I fear none of us could stand against the Mushroom Men. Their touch is death, and even breathing the dust from their bodies would kill us. We must travel through the forest, instead. But it is still a dangerous trek. There are many dangers, and we will have to be mindful of the Temple of the Slug."

She arched her back and put her hands on her hips. My eyes were once again drawn to her breasts, so I glanced quickly at Bloop, who was crouched over the body of one of the Anunnaki, looting the corpse. As I watched, he tried putting on the police riot armor, but his furry, barrel-shaped chest was far too broad to accommodate it. He picked up a fallen handgun, sniffed it, and then tossed the weapon aside. Finally, he settled on a sword. When he looked up and caught us staring at him, he bared his fangs and grinned.

"Bloop!" He thumped his chest again and hefted the sword over his head like a character in some old pirate movie.

"Well," I said, turning back to Kasheena, "I guess he's with us."

"Bloop!" He grunted as if in confirmation.

"And you, Aaron?" Kasheena asked. "What of you? Will you help me to get home? With the promise that when we arrive, Shameal will assist you?"

I would have helped her anyway, regardless of whether or not her tribe's wise man could assist me in getting back home again. Her beauty was reason enough for me to help her. Indeed, it was powerful enough that I would have followed her anywhere, just for the privilege of being in her presence. But I didn't say any of these things. Instead, I bowed, made a sweeping gesture with my arm, and pointed at the path.

"Lead the way," I said.

Her smile was answer enough.

5

STEEL AND SCALE

BEFORE DEPARTING ON OUR JOURNEY, I returned to the tree stump where I'd stashed my gear and retrieved my plastic bag. It took me a few minutes to find it, but my companions were patient.

When I returned, we salvaged the weapons and equipment from the rest of our fallen foes and stripped them of their armor. Then Bloop and I piled their corpses together in a heap. The police riot armor fit me, although it was somewhat loose around my shoulders. The armor reeked of serpent, but I couldn't afford to be squeamish. I donned both it and the matching helmet, and found a dagger that one of the Anunnaki had sheathed in his boot. Testing the blade proved it to be very sharp and finely honed. I wondered if the craftsmanship was that of the snake men, or if the weapon had simply been stolen from one of their captives. There was no detailing or design work on the hilt that might indicate a manufacturer, which I found curious given its expert quality. Shrugging, I added the small blade to my armament of sword and handgun. I considered taking some of the other guns, as well, but they had less ammunition than mine, and I didn't want to overburden myself with extra weapons. Juggling multiple firearms would make them more difficult to carry, and harder to use quickly, if needed. I experimented for a long time with the strange heat rifle but was unable to figure out how to operate it. Neither of my companions was familiar with it, either. Regretfully, I cast it aside.

Kasheena selected one of the pistols and a short sword. When I asked her if she knew how to shoot, she merely smiled at me. None of the armor would fit her or Bloop, but in addition to the sword he'd previously taken, our furry blue companion chose a second blade of equal size and length. He made quite an imposing figure, standing there with one sword hilt in each massive fist—a fuzzy sort of corsair. Judging by what I'd seen of his dexterity so far, I had no doubt he could wield both weapons with accuracy. I wondered idly if he could simultaneously brandish a third sword with his tail, but I had no way of asking, and my attempt to communicate the question via sign language was futile. He merely frowned at me and repeated his name.

I searched through the canvas backpack the last snake man had been wearing. It was in good shape and contained a number of small items—coins, rocks, a small serpent pendant with jade green eyes. The latter made me uneasy to look at, and I tossed it aside. I also got rid of the rocks after a quick examination. Perhaps they'd meant something to their owner, but I saw no discernable value in them. The coins were rough-hewn and crude, with no markings or engravings. The backpack also contained Kasheena and Kasham's clothing, which consisted of fur loincloths. Kasheena put hers on. I tried not to watch, busying myself instead with transferring all of my gear into the backpack.

"Is that all your people wear?" I asked.

She shook her head. "I had more, as did my uncle, but I do not see them in the pack. But no, I do not travel about with only a loincloth. That would be foolish. It does not offer much protection."

It occurred to me that for Kasheena, clothing was a matter of practicality, rather than modesty.

"Will you be okay in just that?"

"I will have to be," she replied, shrugging again. "Perhaps we will find more as we go along."

Finally, we buried Kasheena's uncle. I used one of the leftover swords to dig up the dirt. The soil was soft and rich, and the task was easy enough. There were few roots or rocks to impede my progress. As I dug, I stirred up several insects, worms, and grubs. Some of them were very much like the ones found on Earth. Others were entirely alien to me. Bloop greedily ate handfuls of the grubs, smacking his lips together and grunting with an obvious, if somewhat discomforting, pleasure. When he offered me some, I declined with a polite hand gesture. The ones I'd eaten earlier in the day had been enough for me. Bloop gobbled another handful. He smiled at me, grub pulp dangling from his whiskers. When he'd finished, he and I lowered Kasham into the hole. Then we stood by solemnly while Kasheena hovered over the grave.

"Do your people believe in a Heaven?" I asked when she'd finished her mourning.

"What is Heaven?"

I laughed. "Well, back where I come from, many people ask the same question. Heaven is an afterlife—it's a place we go after we die. At least in spirit."

"Perhaps my people go to Heaven," she said. "I do not know."

"Your people must have some sort of belief about what happens when you die?"

She shrugged. "All I know is that we leave this place. That is what I have always been told, and I believe it to be so. I have seen many people die, and I have never seen them again after that, so they must have indeed left the Lost Level."

"And I'm assuming you bury all of your people after they die? Like we just did for your uncle?"

"Well, of course we do. If we didn't, the animals would eat, pick, and scatter their corpses. Do your people not do the same for your dead?"

"We do," I admitted, "for the most part. But it holds more significance than that. It's a ritual of sorts. A way of saying goodbye to those we care about."

"Bloop," our fur-covered compatriot exclaimed.

"Exactly," I said.

Our conversation faltered as we began our trek through the jungle. When we did talk it was in hushed tones, short snatches of communication regarding the direction we should go. Occasionally, my companions would warn me about certain plants or would halt suddenly, alerted by various jungle sounds. In one case, there was a distinct, light chirp, the kind much like those of the songbirds back home, but the delightfully cheery sound obviously filled Kasheena and Bloop with dread. They crouched in a bed of ferns, both visibly frightened. Both of them motioned at me to get down, so I did. We remained hidden in silence, and neither of them moved again until long after the sound had faded.

"What was it?" I asked.

"A tikka-bird," Kasheena whispered. "Very small, but very dangerous. It is no bigger than your thumb, and most of it is teeth. Their bite is poisonous, and can paralyze their prey within a few heartbeats. When they attack, others like them are drawn by the scent of blood. Such a flock can devour you within minutes, stripping the flesh from your bones."

"So, they're sort of like flying piranha?"

"I do not know these flying piranha, but if they attack and eat anything that moves, then yes. That is like the tikka-bird. Of all the dangers here, I think they are among the worst."

I had a vision in my head of a flying school of piranha with feathers and wings. It seemed ludicrous to me, but Kasheena's dread was apparent. She was clearly shaken, judging by her expression and behavior. I glanced at Bloop. His nostrils were flared, and he scanned the treetops and branches warily.

"Well," I said, "then I hope I never meet one up close."

"If you do, you will probably not live to tell about it, and should you be fortunate enough to escape, it will be without your ears or nose or perhaps your fingers."

We proceeded in silence again for a while. A pall seemed to hang over the jungle. It wasn't until the vegetation began to grow thinner and more sunlight shined through the openings that we talked again. When we did, I asked Kasheena something else that had been on my mind.

"How is it that you speak my language?"

She laughed. "Perhaps it is my language that you speak, Aaron Pace."

I nodded, agreeing that the semantics were correct. "Do all of your people speak English?"

"Is that what you call your language? English?"

"Yes."

"That is what we speak, though we do not call it that. It is a funny word."

"Do you know how your language originated?"

She shrugged. "I only know that we have always spoken it. I assume it was the language of our ancestors."

"So, maybe your tribe came from the same place I did."

"Perhaps. I do not know. I know that my father's father was not our first chieftain. There were several before him. It is said that the first people came here from the sky."

"From the sky? You mean, like in an airplane?"

"I do not know what that is."

"It's a...we have them back on my world. They're a means of transport. Like a chariot."

"I do not know what that is, either."

"A chariot is a cart that people ride in. It's usually pulled by some sort of animal. An airplane is similar to that, I guess, except that it is powered by mechanical means. People sit inside of them and fly through the sky."

She squinted at me, as if trying to determine if I was teasing her. Then she shook her head.

"That is back on your world. We do not have airplane chariots. But our ancestors did not come from elsewhere. They came from the sky. The sky is here, not elsewhere."

"But the sky they came from could have been my sky."

"I do not know. Perhaps. I saw what I thought was a metal bird fly overhead when I was a girl. Maybe instead of a bird, it was one of these airplanes. But I do not know where it came from."

I decided to try another question. "Your uncle's skin was a different color than yours. Is that common in your tribe?"

She nodded, making an expression that seemed to indicate she thought this observation very odd. "We have many different colors. Why? Is that unusual on your world?"

"Not at all," I said. "I'm just trying to determine some things here so that I can better understand. Like where your ancestors originally came from, for example."

"We have never worried much about these things, Aaron Pace. My people are more concerned with important matters, like finding food and defending our village and making offspring."

"Do you...." I faltered, feeling my ears turn hot. "Do you have any...children?"

Hands on her hips, Kasheena tossed her head back and laughed.

"No." She shook her head. "Not yet, for I have not chosen my mate. But I will soon. Already, my people urge me to do so."

"Why have you waited?"

"There are certain things I must do first. There are tasks and feats required of all men and women in our tribe before we can select a mate or before those we choose can offer their consent."

"Like what?"

She shrugged. "I must walk across the fire. Hunt and kill enough to feed the entire village for one night. Nothing too difficult. I have completed many of them already. And until I finish the other tasks, I am content to wait for one who I deem worthy."

"Do you have many...suitors?"

She frowned, clearly not understanding the word.

"Many potential mates," I said. "Do you have many who are interested? Or who you are interested in?"

"A few," Kasheena replied. Her smile grew playful. "But I am in no hurry to make up my mind, no matter how insistent the others in my tribe are."

"Good to know," I said.

Now it was Kasheena's ears which turned red. I noticed her smile grow wider.

It matched my own.

As we continued on our way, Bloop took the lead. Kasheena followed him, and I brought up the rear. More of the jungle gave way to forest, and the breeze became more noticeable. Pausing, I removed my helmet and closed my eyes, relishing the feel of the wind on my face and forehead, cooling my sweat. Then, the breeze brought something less enjoyable—an overpowering and unmistakable stench of feces. Scowling, I put my helmet back on, but it did little to block the smell. Bloop and Kasheena noticed it, as well. Both of their noses wrinkled in disgust, and Bloop coughed. I wondered how sensitive his sense of smell was and what impact this foul odor might be having on him.

As we pressed onward, the stench grew stronger. Soon enough, we discovered the source. A tremendous pile of animal dung lay directly in our path. It was as wide as a full-sized car and taller than I was. A horde of insects buzzed and flitted around the stinking pile. My companions paused in front of it, inspecting the mound. Bloop prodded at the feces with the tip of his sword, dislodging several skeletal remains.

"What the hell made this?" I gasped.

"A dragon," Kasheena answered. "But the pile is not fresh. See? There is no steam coming off it, and the smell is not as strong as it would be had these been recent droppings. The insects have already begun to burrow inside of it. I would say this dragon passed through here several hours ago. We should be safe."

"A dragon?" I repeated, gagging.

"That is what my people call them. Perhaps your people have another name."

"I doubt it. Dragons are a pretty universal concept. But there's no such thing as dragons."

"Of course there are," Kasheena said. "Here is the dung of one. Be thankful we crossed paths only with its dung and not with the dragon itself. Otherwise, we would be part of its next droppings."

I started to respond, when a gleam amidst the feces caught my eye. My attention focused on it. Noticing my curiosity, Bloop dug around with his sword and freed the object. It was a bent and misshapen wheel from a wheelchair—not the common type found in hospitals, but from one of the more expensive kind used by people who are paralyzed or otherwise convalescent and spend their entire lives in such things. A few more wheelchair parts and bits of metal oozed from the feces. I wondered who it had belonged to and how it had gotten here, and more importantly, how it had ended up inside the belly and intestinal tract of a supposed dragon.

This place was full of such quandaries, just like the Jeep I'd discovered the day before, sticking out of a cliff-face. These were only the first two I'd discover, but as time went on, I'd find many more. To write of them all would fill this notebook and leave me no room to complete my story, so these examples will have to do. Suffice to say, I came across castoffs from my world and dozens of other worlds on an almost daily basis. Some were mundane. Others bizarre. Some were as strange to me as a cell phone would be to a caveman. Every day, the flotsam and jetsam of the universe washed up here in this strange dimension, just like I had.

We pressed on again, grateful to be clear of the stench. Kasheena and I continued our conversation as we hiked. I was full of questions about this place, and she was a patient, if bemused, guide. We spoke of the weather patterns and geography. I found that the Lost Level had deserts, snow-topped mountains, and even a vast sea. She did not know what was on the other side of the ocean, nor had she ever stood on its shores, but some among her tribe had. Seasons were something else she was unfamiliar with, and I soon surmised that the Lost Level's various temperate zones remained that way pretty much year round. Another surprise was that her people had no concept of years or days. Some of that was attributable to the fact that they had no clear way to mark the passage of time. With an eternal sun dominating the sky, there was no transition of day to night. Understand this—not only did the sun not set; it never seemed to move at all. If the Lost Level was a planet, then it didn't rotate. The sun kept its same place in the sky, regardless of our location or how much time had passed. As a result, her people marked age by the physical changes in things—the height of a tree, the size of an animal, the number of wrinkles on a face, or the grey in their hair.

I noticed that the constant daylight was already having a similar effect on me. I tried to calculate how much time had passed since I'd slept in the cave and found that I couldn't. I wasn't tired, but I was hungry. Ravenous, in fact. So, I was grateful when we stopped to rest a short while later. We sat under a stand of tall ferns next to a small, cold stream. I removed the police riot armor and helmet, and then washed the dirt and Anunnaki blood from me as best I could. Bloop scaled a nearby tree and returned with three large fruits the size of pineapples. They were round and red, with a soft, almost velvety skin, and the pulp inside had the greenish tint and tiny black seeds of a kiwi. I bit into one and found that it tasted like a grapefruit. When I was finished, I wanted more.

"Never eat more than one," Kasheena warned me, smiling. "Too many of them will make your stomach cramp, and then the dragon will not be the only thing leaving its droppings on the trail. I have seen men and women who could not move for days because they ate too many and were in distress."

"Good to know," I said. "They give you the runs."

"The runs?"

"Where I came from, we call those stomach cramps 'the runs.'"

As if to punctuate this, Bloop stood suddenly and brushed the soil, twigs, and leaves from his fur. Then he walked over to a nearby tree and turned his back to us. Seconds later, a stream of pungent urine arced across the tree trunk. When he was finished, he returned to our spot and washed his hands in the stream. Then, he motioned at us to continue. Grunting, I got to my feet and drank from the creek. I donned my armor, and we started off again. I don't know if it was some quality of the fruit, but I found myself possessed of a renewed energy and spirit.

We found more signs of the dragon's passage a short time later. Several trees had been toppled into the trail—uprooted, rather than snapped off, as if something big had pushed them over. The bark was gouged with deep talon marks. I stood there gaping, stunned by the destruction, and trying to picture an animal big enough to have done such a thing. I was also curious as to why, but before I could ask Kasheena, Bloop sat his swords aside and pulled a small, bloody carcass from the undergrowth. Then, he held it up to the sunlight. It was some sort of mammal, similar to a squirrel, but of a type I certainly hadn't seen back on Earth. I asked Kasheena what it was.

"It is a Slukick," she said. "They live in communal nests in the treetops. The dragon was hungry."

"If they live in a group, then where are the rest of them?"

"In the dragon's belly. This one must have fallen to the ground and escaped its notice. We should not let it go to waste."

"But we just ate not too long ago."

"One cannot live without eating. When there is food, you should not let it go to waste, Aaron Pace. To do so is wrong."

"You know, you can just call me Aaron."

Kasheena frowned. "But is your name not Aaron Pace?"

"Yes, that's my name, but it's my full name. Where I come from, my friends just call me Aaron."

Shrugging, Kasheena turned away. She motioned to Bloop, who without pause, raised the furry corpse to his mouth and bit into the exposed, bleeding flesh. He ripped a mouthful free, chewed thoughtfully, and passed the raw Slukick to Kasheena. I watched, revolted as those beautiful, full lips parted, and she did the same. The sounds she made as she chewed were even worse. Then she offered the raw carcass to me.

"Eat," she insisted. Her mouth was stained crimson, and there was a tiny tuft of fur stuck to her chin. "We have had nothing but fruit. We need meat, as well."

I waved her off. "No, thanks."

"You do not eat meat?"

"Oh, I do. I just prefer to cook it first. It's safer that way."

"My people cook flesh with fire, as well. The job of fire tender is one of the most important in our village. He is tasked with insuring that the flame is never extinguished. But we are not in my village, and we have no means of starting a fire, and we need meat."

Smiling, she took another bite. My stomach lurched as I watched her swallow. Then she licked the blood from her lips, pink tongue sliding and glistening, and my nausea gave way to infatuation once again.

"Okay," I said, flipping up the visor on my helmet. "Good point. Can I have some?"

She handed me the carcass. I tried to ignore how sticky it was, or how the matted fur clung to my fingers. I also ignored the small insects buzzing around, attracted by the corpse. I closed my eyes, thought of sushi, and ate. The meat was tough and stringy, and it tasted terrible. I bit through a strand of gristle, chewed twice, and then swallowed. Finished, I opened my eyes and handed the Slukick back to Bloop.

"Here you go, buddy. It's all yours."

I thought I might throw up, but after a brief struggle, I managed to keep the meat down. The raw flesh felt like a ball of lead in my stomach.

"It is good," Kasheena said, wiping her mouth. "Yes?"

I nodded, still struggling with my gorge. When I could speak again, I said, "I might open a chain of Slukick fast food restaurants if I ever make it back home."

"I do not know what that means, but I suspect you are making fun of me."

"No," I said. "I'm not. I promise. Just making a joke. Let's just say I think I'd prefer my Slukick cooked."

When the meal was finished, we continued on. Occasionally, my stomach gurgled, still trying to decide how it felt about the meat I'd consumed. When I saw Bloop licking dried blood from his talons, my gorge rose again.

For a while, the trek was uneventful. Then we came across a muddy area where the game trail crossed a stream. Signs of the dragon's crossing were apparent along the creek bank. Several massive footprints had been left behind in the soft mud. I marveled at them. Each print was almost as long as I was tall and were embedded several feet deep into the earth. Studying them, I learned that the creature had three toes on each massive foot.

After crossing the stream, Bloop suddenly became alert. His pointed ears twitched, and his nostrils flared. Without a sound, he darted off into the undergrowth and emerged a moment later with a concerned expression. He motioned at us to follow him, so we did. He led us through the foliage to a vast, flattened area where all of the plants had been crushed to the ground. It was obvious that something large had bedded down here, and recently.

"The dragon?" I asked.

Kasheena nodded. Meanwhile, Bloop crouched on his haunches, sniffing the air. The concerned expression remained. When he glanced back up at us, he put a finger to his lips, indicating silence. He stood slowly and motioned at the tree line.

"The dragon is close," Kasheena whispered. "I cannot be sure, but I believe he is indicating that the scent is fresh."

Bloop's nostrils flared again. He growled, low and menacing, staring off into the distance. He clutched one sword in his left hand. His tail entwined around the hilt of the other, gripping it tightly. I placed my hand on his furry shoulder in a gesture of re-assurance. His muscles were bunched tight, and he was trembling, but he didn't push me away.

"Take it easy," I said softly. "It will be—"

Before I could finish, a thunderous roar rocked the forest, shaking the treetops above us. The sound stunned me. I've heard jets taking off, stood next to the railroad tracks as a freight train barreled by, and was even front row center for a Motorhead and Sick of It All concert once, but that roar was the loudest thing I had ever heard.

Bloop sprang to his feet, nearly knocking me over. Kasheena cried out and raised her pistol. I was so startled that I dropped my sword. While I was fumbling to pick it up again, a second bellowing cry rang out. It was impossible for us to determine which direction it was coming from. The sound echoed through the trees, seeming to come from all sides at once.

After a third roar, we noticed a new sound. Bloop and Kasheena frowned, obviously unfamiliar with the noise, but I recognized it at once and was reminded of home. It was the sound of hydraulics—very large and powerful judging by how loud they were.

"We need to find cover," Kasheena said, struggling to make herself heard over the cacophony.

"We're pretty hidden right here," I replied. "Maybe we should stay put."

"We cannot hide in the beast's lair. It could come back at any moment! Come, Aaron. We must find a better place."

Bloop was apparently way ahead of her. Switching his second sword from his tail to his free hand, he bounded into the forest, pausing only to glance over his shoulder and motion at us to follow. We did, running along behind him. We crashed through the foliage. Vines and limbs whipped our faces and thorns pulled at our clothes and skin. As we fled, the roars and hydraulic sounds continued to buffet us. They were so loud that we couldn't tell if we were getting closer to them or farther away. The volume was maddening, and I soon became disoriented. I don't know how long we ran. It felt like an hour but it was probably only minutes. My chest burned from exertion, and my heart pounded in my throat.

Suddenly, Bloop skidded to a halt. I nearly crashed into him, but instead I darted to one side and immediately found myself tottering on the edge of a steep cliff. I cried out, arms flailing helplessly. Rocks fell over the edge and plummeted below. I felt something snake around my waist and yank me backward. I gave a frightened little cry. When I looked down, I realized that it was Bloop's tail.

I breathed a big sigh of relief. "Thanks, my friend."

"Bloop," he responded with a nod.

I turned my attention back to the cliff. The slope had been hidden by thick vegetation, but now that I stood on its edge, I could see a deep, narrow valley below us. But the gorge wasn't what caught my attention. What did were the two opponents who were fighting on the valley floor. I had seen many bizarre things since coming to the Lost Level, but it was at that moment that the full otherworldly *strangeness* of my situation hit me full fold. Below us, engaged in a fierce battle, were a Tyrannosaurus Rex and a giant robot.

The Tyrannosaurus looked like every picture I'd ever seen of one, but I was surprised by how lithe and quick the dinosaur was in real life. Its powerful muscles moved like snakes beneath its hide as it spun, twisted, and fought. It had a massive head, the weight of which was balanced by its long, heavy tail. Its back legs were huge, and its tiny forelimbs seemed small in comparison. Despite their diminutive size, however, they were still powerful. The beast used them to batter and claw at its opponent's metallic hull.

The robot was vaguely humanoid, possessing a head, two arms and legs, two glowing red sensors where eyes would be on a human, and a rectangular slash of a mouth, but it stood even taller and broader than the dinosaur. Its metal body was tarnished and dented in places, and a large patch of rust ran up the back of one of its legs like a bad rash. There was writing on its broad chest plate, perhaps a manufacturer's designation or a model number, but the characters and letters were utterly alien to me. Indeed, I doubted they'd have been recognizable to anyone from my Earth.

Trees swayed overhead as the two titans continued fighting. The sounds of their battle engulfed the valley, drowning out everything else. The dinosaur roared, grunted, snorted, and hissed. Its talons screeched on the robot's hull like fingernails on a chalkboard. From inside the robot came the sounds of overworked hydraulics and gyros and the sonorous thrum of machinery. The two collided over and over again, exchanging fierce blows. Each strike reverberated through the landscape around them, sending rocks and tree limbs hurtling into the chasm below. It felt as if their conflict would rend the very landscape.

The Tyrannosaurus managed to catch the robot's arm in its jaws, but when it bit down, the dinosaur succeeded only in breaking its own teeth. I thought after that the battle might be one-sided, but seconds later, the giant reptile succeeded in shattering one of the robot's sensor eyes. Then, it lashed out with its tail and pivoted on its hind legs, swiveling and knocking the metallic monstrosity to the ground. The entire valley shook as the robot crashed to the earth. The Tyrannosaurus slashed at it with one three-toed foot, but the robot seized the appendage and flipped the dinosaur backward into the foliage. Trees splintered and were uprooted as the dinosaur fell, dislodging boulders and clouds of dirt that rained down upon both the Tyrannosaurus and its foe. The rocks banged against the robot's hull, further denting it.

Both opponents rose slowly, circling one another. The dinosaur roared but sounded weaker than it had before, and it was bleeding from dozens of wounds. It was limping, and as its backside turned toward us, I saw why. A broken tree trunk jutted from its rump. Blood welled around the shaft, running down the beast's leg. The Tyrannosaurus shook its head, as if trying to clear its vision, spraying foamy saliva all around.

The robot whirred and chugged, and a terrible grating sound came from somewhere deep inside of it. Then, black smoke began to seep from between its joints. It lurched forward unsteadily and then took a faltering step toward the panting, weakened

Tyrannosaurus. Despite its wounds, the dinosaur grunted in defiance and planted its feet firmly in the mud. Its tail swept back and forth, smashing through the undergrowth. The damaged robot plodded closer toward it, but then a bright gout of flame erupted from the joints around its leg, followed by more black smoke. A second later, the light in its eyes went out, and it collapsed. The ground trembled once more at the impact. Tree limbs and leaves fell all around us. Rocks tumbled down the hill.

Suspecting that an explosion might follow, I motioned at my companions to get down, but they ignored me, mesmerized by the spectacle and carnage below. The dinosaur crept cautiously toward its fallen opponent, but the wind shifted, blowing the acrid smoke directly into the Tyrannosaurus' face. Grunting, it turned away from the robot, lowered its head, and began to lick its wounds. It growled in frustration, unable to reach the broken length of tree stuck in its back. More blood flowed from around the edges of the trunk.

"We should leave," I whispered. "It's distracted right now. Injured."

"But to reach my home," Kasheena replied, "we must cross down into the valley below. To go around the valley will add at least an extra sleep to our journey and take us into regions even more dangerous than the one we travel through."

I wondered what could be more dangerous than a giant killer robot and an angry, wounded Tyrannosaurus Rex, but it didn't seem like the most opportune moment to ask. Kasheena motioned at Bloop and me to follow her. Then, while the dinosaur was still facing away from us and focused on its injuries, she began crawling backward on her hands and knees, away from the edge of the cliff. Bloop and I did the same, but at that moment, the wind shifted again. Heat billowed up out of the ravine, along with a cloud of acrid, oily smoke. Bothersome as it was at our location, I can only imagine how much more intense it was for the dinosaur. The injured creature turned toward the slope, and roared with surprise upon seeing us.

Despite its wounds, the Tyrannosaurus charged, loping toward us with clear intent. The glare in its eyes reminded me uncomfortably of the Anunnaki we had faced earlier. They'd had that same cold, soulless look. I imagined it was the same expression in a shark's eyes, right before they attacked. Horrified, I realized that I'd become distracted, almost mesmerized by the terror rushing toward me. It was no longer limping. Perhaps shock or anger—or both—had enabled it to ignore its pain. Heedless of its injuries, it was clear that the dinosaur had only one thing in mind—devouring us.

With a cry, Bloop scrambled up a nearby tree, using his tail to clutch both of his swords and all four of his limbs to climb, and scaling it with a speed that belied his size. Kasheena followed him, but when it became clear that she wasn't as agile as our furry companion, Bloop lowered his tail like a rope, dropped the swords, and encircled her waist. Kasheena gave a short, surprised squawk as he bore her up onto a limb. The two of them positioned themselves and then urged me to follow. I glanced back to the dinosaur and was dismayed to see that it had already clawed its way up the cliff. The monstrous head was already even with the ground, and I was only a few yards away from those snapping jaws, close enough that I could see the drool dripping from its massive teeth. The creature's breath was foul—a hot, staggering miasma of rotten meat and that same reptilian musk that had clung to the Anunnaki. I quickly calculated that the beast would reach us before I could climb the tree. Furthermore, I was almost certain that even though it was injured, the enraged dinosaur could almost certainly topple our shelter.

Instead of running, I pulled the .45, remembering that I had six bullets left. I stood my ground, with my feet shoulder-width apart, and raised the weapon, grasping it firmly with both hands. Then, with that car-sized head only yards away from me, I took a deep breath, exhaled, and then squeezed the trigger. The gun bucked in my hands, but my shot was true. The dinosaur's rheumy left eye exploded in a shower of wet pulp and dribbled down its snout and splattered over me and the nearby trees. The beast's anguished cry was terrible, washing over me like a physical force and drowning out the echoes of the gunshot. It snorted once, swiveling its head to look at me with its one remaining eye. I gritted my teeth, lining up a second shot and hoping my luck would repeat itself, when, with a shudder, the creature slipped back down the cliff before I could fire. The beast landed at the bottom, near the smoking, red-hot remains of its former foe, sending a great cloud of dirt and debris swirling up into the air. The tree trunk now jutted from its chest, driven through the monster by the fall. The Tyrannosaurus breathed a few more times and then was still.

"Holy shit!" I stood there gaping, shaking from the adrenaline coursing through my veins. The wet remains of its eye dripped from my hair and chin.

Kasheena cheered and Bloop made excited hooting noises as they clambered down out of the tree. Grinning, I approached the edge with caution and peered down into the canyon again. Immediately, another blast of heat bathed my face. I had time for only one brief glimpse before it became too intense to bear, but in that quick moment, I noticed two things. The first was that the robot's wrecked remains were glowing, lit by some raging internal fire, and almost seemed to be turning liquid, as if it were melting. The second thing I noticed was a fissure in the earth. I don't know if it was caused by the intense heat or perhaps the dinosaur's final plunge, but inside that crack I saw something shiny. Squinting, I peered closer. It was part of an underground metal structure. Of that much, I was sure. Perhaps a tunnel or a bunker, partially exposed to the surface during the ferocity of the battle. Then, I caught a whiff of singed hair, realized that it was mine, and had to step back from the edge.

Kasheena and Bloop approached me. I noticed that Bloop had retrieved his weapons. Both of my companions were overjoyed and impressed by how I'd dispatched the Tyrannosaurus. Bloop slapped me on the back, nearly knocking the wind out of me with one of his sword hilts. He leaped up and down in joy, and I patted his back, returning the gesture. When Kasheena hugged me, her bare nipples rubbed against my chest like perfectly round stones. She didn't seem aware of it, and I certainly didn't mind. But when I felt myself begin to stiffen in response, I gently disengaged from her, blushing. She cocked her head and gave me a puzzled smile.

"Sorry," I murmured.

"You are a strange one, Aaron Pace."

"Yeah, I've been hearing that my entire life."

"Do you not like the touch of another? Or perhaps you prefer the touch of other men? If so, it is okay. My uncle was—"

"No," I interrupted, stammering. "I like your touch...I mean the touch of women...just fine. Not that there's anything wrong with the other, either. I just...you took me by surprise is all. Where I come from, most women don't...at least the women I know don't... I'm not doing a good job of explaining things, am I?"

"You do not like me? You have another woman?"

"No! I like you very much, and I don't have another woman. I just...I need to catch my breath, okay? After all, I just killed a Tyrannosaurus Rex."

"So, now you believe in the dragon," she said. "Now you see."

"I believe I just shot something that was extinct in my world millions of years ago. Beyond that, I don't know what to think. My head is spinning. Like I said, I just need to catch my breath."

She nodded. "We will make camp beyond the other side of the valley. Then, you can tell me of the women in your world."

Smiling, I holstered my .45. "That sounds good. I'd like that. And you can tell me more of your world."

"Come. We will have to find another way down. This area is too hot."

As she led us away, I tried to catch another glimpse of that strange underground structure, but the area below was obscured in smoke. Waves of intense heat wafted against my face. It felt like I'd stuck my head in an oven. I smelled roasting meat, and my mouth watered, making me forget all about the nasty Slukick I'd eaten earlier. As my stomach grumbled, I realized that the delicious aroma belonged to the dinosaur, no doubt cooking below due to its close proximity to the robot. I resolved to keep that in mind if I was ever lucky enough to kill one again. Roasted dinosaur flesh seemed much more appetizing than raw Slukick.

Then I did my best to wipe the gore from my head and face and considered that luck would indeed be involved if I ever killed another.

· 6 ·

UNDER THE LIGHT
OF NIGHT

WE FOLLOWED THE CLIFF'S EDGE, walking until the heat and smoke faded. As I've said, it is hard to tell time here accurately, but I would guess that after another half hour we came to a place where we could climb down. A cove of massive trees resembling the Redwoods of my world clung perilously close to the precipice, and some of their thick roots dangled over the side, forming a natural network of ropes for us to use in our descent. The roots were sticky with some sort of odd sap, and I was worried that—much like most of the things I had so far encountered here—the secretion might be dangerous, but Kasheena assured me it was not. Indeed, I was pleasantly surprised to discover that it had a pine-like aroma, a nice change after smelling dinosaur shit and burning metal for so long. She told me that her people used the sap for a number of different applications, including, I was amused to learn, a form of primitive cologne.

Once we reached the bottom of the canyon, our trek across the valley floor was uneventful. The air was noticeably warmer, due to the close proximity of the fire, but not intolerable. Bloop took the lead, again. Kasheena followed him. A few Slukicks chattered in the tree limbs far over our heads, but none of us bothered to shoot at any of them. As I brought up the rear, I kept glancing in the direction of the robot, expecting a blast of extreme heat or clouds of smoke to round the bend and reach us at any moment, or to see flames racing toward us. Thankfully, none did.

I was still concerned about the robot, though. It had been melting from within. What if it started a fire? Then, it occurred to me that perhaps the robot had been nuclear-powered. If so, there was the potential for a much worse environmental disaster than just a forest fire. But neither Kasheena nor Bloop had seemed concerned.

"That robot was melting," I said, finally.

"You mean the metal giant?" Kasheena asked.

"Yes. In my world, they are called robots. They're machines— artificial constructs. Just like the airplanes I mentioned earlier." I couldn't tell from her expression whether she understood me or not, so I pressed on. "The robot was burning from the inside and melting. I can't help but wonder if we should have done something about that. What if it starts a fire or something? We're in the middle of a forest. That's a bad spot to be if a fire breaks out."

"It will rain soon," Kasheena said. "So, even if a fire should start, the rains will extinguish it."

I glanced up at the clear sky. "How do you know it will rain soon?"

"Do you see that moss?" She pointed to a cluster of blue-tinged moss growing on a nearby boulder. "Normally, it is red. Its coloration changes to that shade of blue when rain is certain. That is another reason why we must find shelter soon."

"Interesting," I murmured, and stopped to inspect the moss. "Some sort of chemical reaction, maybe? In response to the humidity or change in barometric pressure?"

I was trying to sound like I knew what I was talking about, but the truth was, I knew absolutely nothing about meteorology or botany. Even if I had, I soon realized that neither of my companions were impressed by my scientific method. I was still bent over, studying the moss, when Kasheena and Bloop hurried me along.

"The morning our paths crossed," I said as we continued on, "I thought I heard thunder. But no rain followed it, and there were no clouds in the sky. Does that happen often?"

Kasheena nodded. "My people have heard it before, too, but we do not know what causes it or why."

"I'm still concerned that robot may have been nuclear powered."

"I do not know what that means."

"Well, it's a type of energy. In truth, I'd do a bad job of explaining it properly, but it is definitely something to be worried about."

"You worry too much about what is behind, Aaron. Instead, worry about what is ahead."

There was a small footpath on the other side of the valley. It wound up through boulders and crevices and crooked trees. As we began our ascent up the trail, I asked Kasheena about the strange metal structure I'd spotted beneath the valley floor, but she had no knowledge of what it could be.

"There are caves below the surface," she said, "and many different tribes live in them, along with other things—creatures it is better not to speak of. And as I mentioned before, there are some who believe the Anunnaki live beneath the ground, as well. But I have never heard of a cave fashioned from metal. Perhaps it was related to the giant who fought the dragon. Perhaps the giant lived there."

"Maybe," I agreed and let the matter pass from my mind. There was so much bizarreness around me, it was hard to focus on one particular thing. I was trapped on a world with dinosaurs, giant robots, a beautiful barbarian princess, a furry black and blue-hued intelligent cat-thing, piranha birds, abandoned Jeeps and wheelchairs, phantom thunder, carnivorous grass, kleptomaniac vines, savage snake men, perpetual sunlight, meteorologist moss, and a host of other things. Underground metal passageways didn't seem so perplexing or important when compared to some of those.

After reaching the top again, we discovered a small spring bubbling up through some rocks. Bloop knelt and sniffed the water. Apparently satisfied that it was safe, he cupped his hands and drank. Then, Kasheena and I did the same. After a brief respite, we continued on our way and soon found a flat, smooth space on the forest floor on which to make camp. Using our swords, the three of us cut fronds from a palm tree and lay them on the ground to make a bed. We covered these with soft green and yellow ferns. After that, we cut some more palm fronds and fashioned a canopy above the bed.

Bloop disappeared into the forest while Kasheena and I gathered a number of large rocks and formed a stone fire pit. I asked her how we would make a fire. To the best of my knowledge, neither her nor Bloop had a tinder box or matches (if they had, I don't know where they would have hidden them, given his full nudity and her lack of anything other than a loincloth). And I certainly couldn't start one with the few items I had scavenged.

Kasheena gave me a playful smile. "I have much to teach you, Aaron."

She walked into the forest and beckoned me to follow. Puzzled, I did as she requested. She searched the ground, overturning rotten logs and sweeping the vegetation aside until she found a strange-colored rock—grey and silver shot through with brick-red speckles. The stone was roughly the size of a baseball. She pried it up out of the ground and then searched until she found another.

"These rocks produce a spark when ground together. I noticed that there were many of them in the area when we were setting up the camp. Unlike our meal before our encounter with the dragon, we can cook our dinner now."

"I'd like that."

"As would I," she agreed. "Gather some tinder, and then I will start a fire. It should give us some comfort until the rains come."

"And how soon will that be?"

She glanced up at the treetops and shrugged. "It is hard to know for sure. The trees grow close together here, and I cannot get a good view of the sky. But soon, I think."

I went about gathering an armful of twigs and branches, mindful of where I stepped and what I touched. I also made sure to focus only on dead wood, rather than cutting any from the trees. I'd seen what some of the vegetation in the Lost Level could do, and I didn't want to take any chances with the strange plants growing around me. I piled the tinder up and then added some of the scrap paper I'd collected from the Jeep.

Bloop returned to camp just as I did. He carried three rabbits with him. They looked remarkably like the rabbits back home, except for their fur, which had a greenish tint—probably some sort of camouflage effect. He proceeded to skin and field dress them. Given my reaction to our earlier meal, I wondered if this was for my benefit or not. He offered us the bloody innards, but both Kasheena and I declined. Shrugging, Bloop noisily slurped them down. Bits of gore dangled from his whiskers and the fur on his chin. He grinned, flashing blood-stained fangs.

Kasheena, meanwhile, piled my tinder in the center of the ring of stones and then crouched over it, holding one of the peculiar rocks in each hand. She struck them together, reminding me of a teacher knocking two chalkboard erasers together, but instead of producing a cloud of dust, a shower of bright sparks erupted. Their vibrancy surprised me. I had expected a few singular sparks, much like that produced from a piece of flint, but instead, it was like she'd turned on an arc-welder. The paper caught fire instantly, and Kasheena knelt over it and blew gently, further fanning the flames until the tinder caught. Twigs popped and crackled as the fire spread. Soon, its heat filled our campsite.

"We will keep these," Kasheena said, hefting the stones. "This type of rock is rare in the lands around my village. My people will be very pleased to receive them. Usually, we must travel far to secure them. May we carry them in your pack, Aaron?"

"Of course."

"We will wrap them in the skins of the rabbits Bloop caught. That will keep the stones from accidentally striking one another and setting your pack on fire. We will clean the skins and let them dry over the fire while we sleep so that the smell of blood doesn't attract predators."

We spitted the rabbits and then roasted them over the fire. As they cooked, my mind wandered back to the smell of the dinosaur roasting in the valley, which then made me wonder again about the possibility of a forest fire breaking out. I touched upon my concerns with Kasheena, but she didn't seem perturbed by the prospect and merely assured me once again that it would soon rain. I also tried to explain my concerns about the nuclear potential of the robot and what impact a meltdown could have on the environment, but was unable to properly articulate it in a way that made her understand my fears.

Conversation dwindled and our impatience grew as we waited for the meat to cook. I occupied myself by sorting through my pack again. First, I used the rest of John LeMay's paperwork to wipe down my .45 and sword, doing my best to clean them with my meager implements. I tossed the soiled papers into the fire, watching the last remnants of John LeMay's life blacken and curl as the flames licked at them. I felt as if I should toast him or something, wherever he was now.

Here's to you, John LeMay, I thought. *You saved my life. I hope somebody did the same for you.*

When the papers were reduced to ashes, I turned my attention back to my gear. I double checked my ammunition and verified that I had five bullets left. Kasheena and Bloop watched with interest as I sorted through everything else. Bloop was especially fascinated with the binoculars and hooted with delight after I showed him how to work them. Kasheena was enamored with the tube of cherry-flavored lip balm. I applied some to my lips and then invited her to do the same to her own. She put some on, licked it off, laughed, and then applied another layer.

Finally, the rabbits finished cooking. All three of us ate ravenously, and I suspect that Kasheena's and my table manners were probably just as bad as Bloop's. Grease dribbled down my chin and forearms, making my beard and arm hair sticky. Fat burst and crackled deliciously beneath my teeth. The meat was burned black on the outside and still half-raw at the center, and it seared my fingers and tongue, but despite that, it was one of the best things I've ever tasted. As I sit here writing this account inside the abandoned school bus, my mouth still waters at the memory of that meal.

And the rabbit isn't the only thing from that night that I remember with such clarity.

After we were finished with our meal, Kasheena dug a hole and buried the rabbit bones so they wouldn't attract predators. Then, using sign language, she indicated to Bloop that he should sleep while we took first watch. After a few moments, our furry companion seemed to get the message. He crawled under the canopy of palm fronds and was soon fast asleep. He snored softly, and he must have dreamed, because occasionally his tail twitched, snaking back and forth behind him. He reminded me of a napping housecat, curled up in the sunshine. Once, he stirred, swatting at a buzzing insect, but then lay still again. Kasheena and I watched him sleep for a while. Then we tiptoed away from the fire and campsite so that we could talk more freely without waking him.

We found an area where the ground had been carpeted by a soft blanket of moss, and we sat down cross-legged and facing one another. Our knees were only inches apart, and occasionally we would accidentally brush against each other. Every time this happened, I felt an electric thrill run through my body. Despite her rugged lifestyle, Kasheena's skin was silken soft. And warm. I remember her warmth most of all. We talked for what felt like hours. I told her of life back on Earth and she told me about life here in the Lost Level. I studied her while we talked—trying hard to not be obvious about it. She had a raw, pure beauty that didn't rely on cosmetics or hair styling or fashion. Her teeth were white, if a tiny bit crooked, but that only added to her appeal. Her hair was clean, and given our close proximity, I inhaled her natural, intoxicating scent with every breath.

At some point, our conversation faltered. I looked into her eyes. She smiled. An instant later, we fell into a passionate kiss. We made love to each other right there on the moss, and halfway through, it began to rain. Kasheena laughed softly as she rode me.

"You see, Aaron? I told you it would rain."

I nodded, reaching up to massage her rain-slicked breasts. She lowered herself and kissed me again. The campfire sputtered and hissed before fizzling out completely. Our lovemaking continued, and soon we were drenched, both from passion and the weather. Concerned about birth control, I attempted to pull out at the last minute, but Kasheena wrapped her arms and legs around me and locked her hips, urging me on.

Later, we crept back into camp and lay down near Bloop. I shook him gently until he awoke and then tried to communicate that it was his turn on watch. Kasheena had already fallen asleep. He glanced at her and then looked at me. His nostrils flared. He grinned, flashing his fangs, and then playfully punched my shoulder. I returned the gesture, even as I felt my ears turn red from embarrassment. Still smiling, Bloop grunted and then moved to the edge of the shelter. With his weapons within easy reach, he sat cross-legged and stared out into the rain.

I curled up next to Kasheena, spooning her, and tried to sleep. I'd feared that sleeping during perpetual daylight might prove difficult, but it didn't with her by my side. I closed my eyes and sighed. My last thought was a feeling of contentment and gratitude, and a vague sense of disquiet when I considered my eventual return to Earth.

I awoke at some point, unable to guess how much time had passed. I felt groggy and found it hard to focus at first, so it couldn't have been too long. The first thing I became aware of was that the rain had stopped. It occurred to me that I hadn't noticed if the sky got darker with the arrival of the storm clouds, preoccupied as I'd been, and now it was too late to tell. The sun beat down upon us, as always. The cooler temperatures the storm had brought with it were gone now, dissipating like the steam rising up from the ground.

The forest was now filled with the sound of water droplets falling from the trees, but that wasn't what had disturbed me from my sleep. What had woken me was a second sound—a low, distant rumbling that sounded unmistakably like a machine. Despite the heat and sunlight, the sweat on my body turned cold and the hair on my arms stood up. Fearing that another giant robot was approaching our camp, I bolted upright, gasping.

Bloop turned, startled by my reaction. He cocked his head, staring at me with a puzzled expression. I pointed to my ear, but his confusion was still apparent. I held a finger to my lips, indicating silence, and then cupped my ear as if listening. The machine sounds hadn't grown louder, but now that I was aware of them, I could hear them more clearly. They were a distinct, steady throbbing noise, similar to an idling engine. Curiously, it seemed to be coming from beneath our feet. Then I became aware that the trees around us were swaying slightly, and yet there was no breeze. Whatever it was, it was enough to disturb them from below.

I made a listening motion again and then pointed at the ground. Bloop cocked his head and then shrugged. I repeated the hand signals more insistently. Sighing, Bloop got to his feet and padded over to me. He pointed at the ground, then his ear.

"You hear it, too, don't you?"

I know he didn't understand me, but my tone must have communicated my intent, because Bloop nodded and then shrugged. Then he put his hands together, lay his furry cheek against them and pretended to sleep. When he opened his eyes again, he pointed at me and then back to the shelter, where Kasheena still slept undisturbed.

"But what is it?" I asked. "What's that noise? Aren't you concerned? What if it's another one of those giant robots?"

Bloop commiserated by making a low murmuring growl. Then, he gave my shoulder a gentle pat and indicated once again that I should go back to sleep. Sighing with frustration, I crawled back to bed while Bloop returned to his post. I lay there listening to the machine sounds and wondering about their origins. Eventually, the noise ceased, but it was a long time before I slept again.

7

THE FINAL FATE
OF FLIGHT 19

THERE'S NO WAY OF TELLING how much longer we slept. It could have been only hours or it could have very well been days. I awoke to find that Kasheena had already risen. She had managed to light another fire and was in the process of cooking breakfast. I was surprised to see Bloop curled up nearby me, snoring softly. Obviously, enough time had passed that she'd relieved him on watch. When I asked her about this, I was stunned to discover that each of them had stood two additional watches while I slept.

"I did not want to wake you," Kasheena said. "You slept so soundly, and it seemed a shame to disturb it. I thought perhaps you needed time to recover from the shock of being away from your people. So, we let you sleep."

"I can't believe I slept that long," I replied with some embarrassment. "Time travel must have really worn me out."

"Time travel? Is that what you call your journey from your world to here?"

Shrugging, I moved over to join her by the fire. The heat felt good, despite the already warm temperature of the air. "Well, some might call it time travel, although I would guess that the term dimensional travel might be more appropriate. The methods I used to arrive here allowed me to move through both space and time."

I could tell by her expression that she didn't understand me, so I tried to explain it. As I did, I found that talking it out helped me come to terms with my situation, as well.

"This wise man from your tribe—"

"Shameal."

"Yes," I replied. "Shameal. Back home, I guess I was sort of like him. I was interested in magic. The occult. I studied it and practiced it, and that's how I ended up here."

"You were a wise man?"

"Well, I don't know how wise I was if I ended up getting shipwrecked in another dimension."

"I still do not understand this word—time travel."

"There are different worlds other than this one," I said. "Different places where people live."

She nodded. "This I know."

"Time passes in each of those worlds. You mark its passage differently here, but your people still have a concept of time. You judge it by sleeps or the changes a person undergoes as they grow older."

"Yes."

"Now, each of those worlds also has different versions of themselves existing in parallel dimensions. Some call those dimensions levels. Things don't exist in them at the same time together. In my studies, I read of your world—the Lost Level. This is a place—a dimension—where things from all those other worlds can end up stranded at the same time. That explains all the different flora and fauna—the plants and animals. You don't see them as strange because you've lived here all of your life, but from my perspective, it is unusual to see them all together in one place. The rabbits we had for dinner last night versus the thing you called a dragon yesterday. In my world, they don't exist at the same time. The dragons died out millions of years ago, long before rabbits flourished. But here, in your world, they exist side by side. Or take all the things I've found since my arrival. Before I rescued you and Bloop, I came across a vehicle—something my people use for transport—embedded in a cliff. That's from my time. But some of those weapons the Anunnaki were carrying must have come from the future, given how advanced they were. Or, it's even a possibility that they didn't come from my world at all."

"Like some of the things in your pack," she said. "When I retrieved the rocks from your bag to start the fire, I glanced at them. I do not know what some of them are, but I know they are not magic. The things you lent to Bloop yesterday, that allow a viewer to see far away—"

"Binoculars."

"Yes. Ben-ock-you-larz. Some in my tribe would think them magic, but after studying them, I can see that they were made by humans. They are a tool. Nothing more. A wondrous tool, but a tool all the same. It would take a long time for someone to make them, so they are from the future?"

"Sort of," I replied. "My present, but your future, perhaps. If your people invent a whole bunch of other things first."

"And when you say you are a wise man, do you mean that all of your magic is like these binoculars?"

"Not really. But there are some on my world who say that magic is simply science we don't yet understand, so perhaps?" I paused, considering. "Yes, perhaps it is after all."

Nodding, she turned her attention back to the fire for a moment. She had suspended a large stick above the flames. Hanging from it were three tubular roots that resembled a cross between a potato and a carrot.

"What are those?" I asked.

"My people call them squatosh. They are not from the future. I dug them up while you and Bloop were sleeping. That means they are from the past and have traveled through time."

It took me a moment to realize that she was joking. Grinning, I scratched the back of my neck and shook my head. "I guess I kind of deserved that."

"We should wake Bloop," she said, still smiling. "Our meal will be ready soon. It is a shame. I had hoped we could be together again before he awoke."

She bent over the fire, swaying her hips back and forth, and I went to her, encircling her waist with my arms.

We decided to let Bloop sleep a little bit longer, after all.

The roasted squatosh was delicious, with a taste and texture much like a sweet potato. It was also surprisingly filling. I'd anticipated still being hungry upon finishing mine but instead found myself pleasantly full, as if I'd just eaten a bowl of oatmeal. Bloop was indifferent about his. I couldn't figure out if that was because he preferred meat or if he was just not a morning person. The thought made me crave a hot cup of coffee to wake up with, but when I asked Kasheena if her people had such a beverage, she looked at me strangely and explained the only hot drinks they served were for medicinal purposes and tasted bitter.

"Here's hoping a Starbucks gets sucked through the space-time continuum and ends up here," I said.

"Starbucks?"

"Never mind. Just something from back home."

We put out the fire and packed up camp and then started on our way. Once again, Kasheena guided us in the direction of her village, and I marveled over her apparently uncanny sense of direction. When we came across a wide, swift-moving stream, we stopped. After Bloop had verified that the water was safe to drink, I filled up my travel mug. Then we waded across the stream.

The water was cold and shallow, reaching only to my ankles in most places and up to my knees at the deepest point. The current was swift, but not overpoweringly strong, and it would have been easy to stand if not for the slippery rocks beneath the surface. They were covered with small, black-shelled barnacles and different types of algae and plants—everything from fronds of what looked like kelp to thousands of strange, translucent tubers that resembled miniature jellyfish. There were also dozens of tiny brown fish. They looked remarkably like brook trout, but smaller. Kasheena and Bloop did not react to them, so I assumed they were safe as they darted around our plodding feet. I saw no trash or foreign debris—no broken glass bottles, rusty tin cans, discarded fishing lures, or any of the other things I might find in the streams back on Earth. I did, however, see a rock beneath the surface that looked like either a fossilized brain or a sponge. It was about the size of a soccer ball, and when I picked it up, I was surprised by how light it was. Upon closer examination, I determined that it was indeed a fossil, but I didn't know of what. Reluctantly, I dropped it back into the creek. It made a loud splash, and Bloop scowled at me with gentle reproach.

After crossing the stream, we continued on our trek through the forest, sticking to game trails when they were available and beating our way through the underbrush when they weren't. Time passed uneventfully. We didn't encounter any more dinosaurs or robots or snake men. Indeed, we didn't encounter much of anything at all. The trees were alive with bird songs and the chatter of small animals, but for the most part, the wildlife itself remained out of sight. It was uneventful enough that I almost found myself lulled into complacency, but each time my attention wandered, I remembered some of the dangers that lurked all around and focused again on our surroundings.

After several hours, the vegetation around us began to change. I noticed many new species of trees and bushes, the likes of which I had never seen before. I wondered what world they were from or if they were perhaps native to the Lost Level. I also found myself considering the vegetation in general. Some of the plants were undoubtedly from my world or others like it. Others definitely weren't. How had they come here from their individual levels? Had they been carried by castaways such as myself? Or perhaps their seed pods or saplings had been transported here? And how, I wondered, could I tell what the native flora was and which were from another world? Indeed, when it came to flora and fauna, was any of it native to this realm? Or had it all come from elsewhere, just as I had? Sure, Kasheena had been born here, so she was certainly native, but what of the roots of her tribe? Where had they come from originally? Was everything in the Lost Level part of the dimensional flotsam and jetsam?

Different worlds, different dimensions—they all occupied a specific place in space and time. Physical locations like Earth or Mars, or metaphysical realms such as Heaven or Hell or the Void, all of them existed in a specific place, accessible by specific means. But what space did the Lost Level occupy? And if it was possible to breach its space and to be transported here, then why was the reverse not true? Why, supposedly, were we unable to leave?

We clambered up a steep hillside that was covered with tall, brown grass and several short, stunted bushes that jutted sideways from the rocky soil. At the top of the hill, we found the remains of a stone wall. It had collapsed in places, and moss and weeds jutted from between the cracks. I wondered aloud who had built it, but Kasheena did not know.

"I heard something," I said as we hiked. "While you were sleeping during our last camp. Bloop heard it, too."

"What was it?"

"It sounded like machines, far beneath the ground. Do you know what they were?"

"My people have heard them from time to time," Kasheena replied. "As has anyone who lives in this land. They sound like the giant metal man, yes?"

I nodded.

"I do not know what makes the sound," Kasheena said. "When we were little, Shameal told us that the sounds were made by the Creator."

"The Creator...you mean some type of supreme deity?"

"The Creator is the one who made this land."

"But when we first met, you said your tribe believes everyone in this land came from elsewhere."

"Yes, that is true. The Creator made the Lost Level, but not the things that live in it. Those came from elsewhere, like you, or were born here, like me."

"And you worship this Creator god?"

Kasheena laughed. The sound was light and musical.

"Worship the Creator? No. No one has ever seen the Creator. How can you pay tribute to something you cannot see? The Creator simply is."

"Okay." I was intrigued. "Tell me more about this Creator."

"There is not much more to tell, Aaron. We do not think about the Creator. We do not see the Creator. We never speak with the Creator. The Creator simply is. When you hear the rumblings beneath the Earth? That is the work of the Creator. Shameal says it is better not to ask questions about the Creator and to simply let it be."

I had more questions, but Kasheena had no answers. She patiently rebuffed my requests until I gave up in frustration. Instead, I let her point out edible plants and roots to me while I slapped at insects. I noticed Bloop swishing his tail back and forth to chase the bugs away, much like a horse or cow would do back home.

We descended the hill and entered a broad ravine with a dry creek bed in its center. The treetops grew close together overtop the gulch, casting a perpetual shadow. The ravine walls were covered with sprawling growths of ivy and vines, and after Kasheena had guided us a few hundred yards, I noticed something jutting from the undergrowth. It was a rusted section of airplane fuselage with the numbers 45714 and FT3 painted on it. I rushed over to the hulk and cleared the vegetation away with my sword, revealing the battered shell of a World War II era TBM Avenger torpedo bomber. As a child, I'd often built model airplanes with my grandfather, so I knew the aircraft well.

I glanced around the ravine and noticed more derelicts, each of which was nearly hidden beneath the ivy. I began hacking at the vines with my sword. Kasheena and Bloop watched me as if I'd lost my mind and then began to help. Bloop swung both swords, making quick work of it. Soon, we stood there panting and covered in sweat, staring at the remains of five TBM Avengers. Four of them were TBM-1C models, and the fifth was a TBM3. The paint on their fuselage was faded, muddy, and eaten through with rust, but the numbers were still legible on four of the planes—FT36, FT81, FT117, and FT28. The fifth was too faded to read. The numbers were familiar to me, but I couldn't figure out why. After a few moments, I realized what they were, and my skin broke out in gooseflesh, despite the heat.

"Holy shit," I exclaimed. "It's Flight 19!"

"I have seen a thing like these before," Kasheena said, "but it was a long time ago, when I was a little girl."

"You mentioned that once before, but you never had the chance to finish telling me about it."

"It flew over my village like a strange metal bird before crashing in the jungle."

"Was there anyone inside of it?" I asked.

She shook her head. "It burst into a ball of flame. When the men from our tribe went to investigate, they said there was nothing left. I remember that it burnt down a swath of the forest, and many were worried that we might have to flee. But our people dug ditches to halt the fire's advance, and eventually it burned itself out."

"Do you remember anything else?"

"No. As I said, I was very little. I always thought it was a bird."

Approaching the closest plane, I ran my hand across a .30 caliber machine gun which was mounted in the nose. I doubted that the weapon was still functional. The barrel was rusty and insects had made nests inside of it. Obviously, it had been here for some time.

"What is this Flight 19?" Kasheena asked. "Were they vehicles?"

"Yes," I said, thinking back to my years of research into the paranormal. "Very famous vehicles. These are called airplanes, like we talked about before. They're machines that flew through the air, just like the one you saw when you were little. These numbers painted on the side correspond to Flight 19, which was a group of airplanes that disappeared on December 5, 1945 during a training flight off the coast of Florida—that's a state in America, the place where I'm from. Each plane had a three-man crew—a pilot, a gunner, and a radioman. The pilot flew the plane, the radioman was in charge of communicating with people on the ground, and the gunner was the fighter. He would shoot at enemy planes."

"So, where are the men who flew in these airplanes?"

"I wish I knew. So do many people back where I come from. See, Flight 19 was a famous disappearance, connected to something we called the Bermuda Triangle—an area of the ocean where many people have vanished over the years. I must have read a dozen books about this when I was younger. I was nuts about the whole thing."

"Maybe those people who vanished in this Triangle came here," Kasheena said.

I nodded. "The crew of Flight 19 did, at least. The flight leader was..." I searched my memory, trying to recall the name. "Lieutenant Charles Tyler? Or Taylor, maybe? Yeah, I think Taylor was his name. Some people believed it was his fault the planes disappeared. He showed up late the morning of the training mission, and he made some confusing and strange decisions while they were in the air. There was a theory that he might have become disoriented, and then he ordered his men to ditch the planes into the ocean after they ran out of fuel, and everyone bailed out. Obviously, that didn't happen."

"Could these airplanes still work?" Kasheena asked. "Our journey would be much easier and safer, I think, to travel in one. How amazing that would be, to travel across the sky!"

I shook my head. "No, these are long past working. And even if they were still functioning, I don't know how to fly one. You need special training for that."

"But you have proven capable many times, Aaron. Surely, you could do this, as well."

I chuckled softly. "I wish. But sadly, no."

We searched each of the aircrafts, but exposure to the elements had left nothing salvageable amongst the wreckage. Some kind of animal had nested in one of the cockpits. It was filled with sticks and matted leaves. The nest had been abandoned, but it had a musky scent that I found unsettling. In all of the planes, the seats were torn and covered with mold and grime, and most of the metal had rusted. There were no skeletons or other signs of human remains, nor were there any scraps of uniforms or survival packs. That meant one of two things. Either Lieutenant Taylor and his men had abandoned the planes and ventured out into the forest, or they had died here and the site had been looted and time had erased all existence of their remains. Judging by the position of the planes, they hadn't crashed, but I couldn't imagine how they'd managed to land them in the ravine without incident. Maybe whatever event it was that had transported them here deposited them in the ravine upon arrival. But if they had survived, where were they now? Were they even alive? Judging by their condition, the Avengers had been here for a very long time. So had the pilots, if they were still alive. How old would Taylor and his men be now? I didn't know how to tell time in the Lost Level, but I knew how to mark its passage—the stubble on my face or the length of my fingernails indicated that time still passed normally here, just like it did back home. If Flight 19 had indeed landed here in 1945, then they would be old men by now.

I weighed the possibility that they had landed here more recently. Perhaps it had still been 1945 in their world when they vanished, but their arrival here in the Lost Level had been merely a few years or months before my own. Given the nature of time travel, this was plausible, but when I considered the condition of the airplanes themselves, I found it the most unlikely scenario. Which brought me back to speculating on the whereabouts of the crew. Had they made a life for themselves here, perhaps building a permanent shelter? If so, could any of them still be alive?

Or maybe it was possible that they'd found a way back to our world. Or their world. There was no guarantee that this particular Flight 19 was even from my reality. It could just as easily originated from an alternate universe—an alternate Earth. Maybe they'd found a way to return there, albeit without their planes. If so, then—despite legend saying it was impossible—that meant that I could do the same. I could find a way to return to my own level and escape this place once and for all. The possibility didn't excite me as much as it should have, and I paused to wonder why.

I turned to Kasheena. "I'm assuming that no one from your tribe has ever mentioned this place? Or the planes?"

"No. If so, then it was before my time, and our elders have never spoken of it to us. I have only been this way a few times, and there was never time for exploration on those trips. The landscape will become more familiar to me after our next sleep."

I nodded, turning my head to scan the forest.

"Are you okay, Aaron? You seem troubled."

"I'm still wondering what happened to the men who flew these craft," I said. "Wondering if they are alive or...dead. Wondering if they made it back home. Do you know of any other settlements or villages nearby?"

"No. In this area, it is just ours."

I nodded again, still staring at the trees.

"We should move on," Kasheena suggested. "There is nothing here for us, and I do not like this place. It feels sad."

Nodding in agreement, I climbed down from the plane, and we continued on our way. I glanced back only once, and when I did, Flight 19 had already vanished again, swallowed once more by the undergrowth.

And by time.

8

GREY WATER

OUR JOURNEY PASSED UNEVENTFULLY FOR a while
after that. At times, it felt to me as if we were wandering in circles.
The terrain didn't change much, although Kasheena seemed to
recognize various distinct features and landmarks. She seemed
positive that we were still on track for her village, and getting closer. I had no choice but to trust her instincts. Bloop seemed okay
with this arrangement, as well. Most of the time he stayed with us.
Occasionally, he would bound off into the underbrush in pursuit
of wild game. Then he'd return, happy and gloating, and usually
with something for us to eat. In some ways, he reminded me of a
big dog. He was certainly as committed and faithful a companion
as a dog, but obviously far more intelligent. I wondered what his
story was and wished he could tell us. Were there more of his
people here in the Lost Level, or, like me, was he a dimensional
castaway? Did he have a mate? Children? Parents, perhaps? Was
there someone back home missing him?

That thought made me consider my own family. Only once
since my arrival in the Lost Level had I considered how my disappearance might be impacting them. I hadn't exactly been
close with them over the last few years, devoting my time to my
occult studies and other pursuits, as I had. But I'd stayed in
touch with my siblings online and called my parents every Sunday afternoon, and we all got together during the big holidays.
The last time I'd seen them in person had been the week between Christmas and New Year's, when we'd all stayed at my
parents' home. Most of our discussions then had been polite

but guarded, the conversation of people who didn't have much in common anymore but still shared a history. But despite that distance, I loved them, and I think they loved me. Would they notice I was gone by now? Indeed, I wondered how much time had passed back on my Earth. Was time there the same as here in the Lost Level, or was it different? It would have been presumptuous of me to assume that time passed the same in both dimensions. While I had only been here a few days (or whatever passed for days in a place where the sun never set), entire decades or even centuries might have passed back home. Or perhaps only a few minutes or seconds. If I was ever successful in making it back to my Earth, it was possible I might find that I'd long been given up for dead by those who had known me. It was equally possible that I'd discover I had barely been gone in the time it takes to blink. Thinking about all of the different possibilities made my head hurt.

As we hiked, Kasheena and I continued our discussions about the Lost Level. I learned more about its ocean and desert regions and was very surprised to discover that it even had frozen areas with regular arctic-like conditions, despite the presence of an eternal sun hanging overhead. Other than the snowfall on some of the mountaintops, I had assumed the entire dimension was as temperate as the forests and jungles I'd experienced so far, but that wasn't so. I was especially curious to know more about the Creator and anything more concerning the Lost Level's subterranean features, but unfortunately, Kasheena didn't know much. She insisted several times that she had told me everything she knew about what lay beneath our feet. As for the Creator, her people believed that the Creator was just that—an entity who had created the Lost Level. It had no sex or gender, at least not that she knew of, nor were there any fables or legends surrounding it. There was no dogma and no set of rules or commandments dedicated to or derived from its worship. She knew of no identifiable characteristics. According to her, the mysterious figure didn't even have a name, other than the Creator, which she admitted was a name her people had given it. Other inhabitants of the Lost Level had different names and theories for the unknown entity.

Sometimes, we encountered signs of other intelligent life. Once, we found what appeared to be Native American petroglyphs carved

into the exposed face of a large boulder. The crude diagrams depict-
ed everything from beavers, deer, and snakes to dinosaurs, flying
saucers, and what was almost certainly an Anunnaki. Kasheena had
no knowledge of them and no idea who might have made them or
how long they'd been there. Another time, we found Chinese letters
scratched into a tree trunk. These she had known about and said
that while she had never seen them for herself, a hunter from her
tribe had spoken of them. Apparently, they'd been there for a long
time.

Occasionally, we also came across random dimensional relics
that reminded me of home. There was nothing as impressively
awe-inspiring as the wreckage of Flight 19, or as bizarre as a Jeep
fused with a mountainside or a partially-digested wheelchair buried in dinosaur shit. Some of the things I found weren't even
from Earth, mine or any other, but the ones I recognized were
comfortable in their familiarity, all the same—a pair of scissors
half-buried in the dirt, a broken television, a frayed dog collar, an
empty disposable cigarette lighter, a pair of hospital crutches, a
cracked child's wading pool with faded animal characters painted
on the sides of it, a cell phone charger, a doll with a missing arm
and eye, a rubber gasket, plastic bottles and dented aluminum
cans (because apparently even parallel dimensions had pollution),
an automobile license plate from the United Kingdom, a dirty and
weathered Chinese takeout menu whose lettering was so faded
that I couldn't make out where it was from, a department store
mannequin, a red yo-yo with Japanese writing on it, an empty canister of bug-spray, a glass Mason jar with a chip on the rim, a jumble of parts that I thought might have come from a propane grill,
a Civil War-era powder can with a bullet hole in it, and a steel-
belted radial complete with a chrome rim that had become the
nesting place for a family of small lizards. All of these items appeared to have been here for a long time, and none of them were
really salvageable.

I thought Bloop might enjoy the yo-yo, so I cleaned the dirt
off of it and tested it out. I was surprised to find that the string
was still strong and resilient, and not nearly as frayed or weather-
worn as I'd assumed it would be. I then ran through my rather
meager repertoire of tricks with it. Bloop seemed interested
enough and laughed as I did Walk the Dog, Sleeper, and Around

the World. Kasheena smiled dubiously, watching us both. I did a few more tricks, and Bloop clapped, so I handed the yo-yo to him. He tried to repeat the tricks, but the string became tangled almost instantly. Growling with frustration, he brought the yo-yo to his nose and sniffed it. Then he tried to untangle the string but only succeeded in making it worse. Next, he put the toy in his mouth and tried to bite it. His teeth clacked against the hard plastic. With a grunt, he hurled the toy into the forest.

I grinned. "Maybe we can find you a Playstation or an Xbox, instead."

Bloop snorted at me, and then scratched his groin. We continued on our way. The police riot armor grew heavy, chafing my shoulders. The backpack didn't help. I considered jettisoning some of my gear—things like the compact discs and other assorted items from John LeMay's Jeep, but after thinking about it, I decided to hold on to them a while longer. They might still prove useful, I reasoned. But I also wondered if it was their practicality that made me keep them, or the fact that they reminded me of home. And, in truth, they weren't that much of a burden. Dropping them wouldn't have noticeably decreased the weight I was carrying. I glanced at Bloop, clutching one sword in his left paw and wielding the other with his tail, and wished I had an extra prehensile appendage to help lessen my load.

When we got tired, we stopped and made camp again. After building a fire and eating a meal together, I volunteered to take the first watch. After Bloop was asleep, Kasheena and I made love twice. Then she went to sleep, as well. I stroked her hair for a while, then got up and sat cross-legged near the fire. Falling asleep on watch wasn't a concern—not the way my mind was spinning. I thought back over the events of the past few days, which led me to return to the train of thought I'd had earlier and ponder the idea of days themselves. At that point, I was really struggling with how to mark the passage of time. It had never occurred to me just how reliant we were—as a species—on calendars and schedules. When I attempted to calculate just how long I'd been trapped in the Lost Level, my only frame of reference was how many times I'd slept. It seemed so strange, but as I pondered it more, I wondered if this style of living might not be better. There was a certain freedom in not being beholden to the cycles of the sun, or a time clock, or a busy social calendar—to sleep only when tired and awake only after the body was sufficiently rested, rather than the obtrusive blaring of an alarm clock.

When the fire began to dim, I added some more wood to it. Then, I tended to my gear. Using some broad, green leaves, I wiped down my police riot armor and helmet and sat them aside to air out. Then I cleaned my dagger, sword, and handgun. Using the reflective side of one of the compact discs I'd scavenged from the Jeep, I studied my reflection. It was strange, seeing myself with a beard and longer hair. Even stranger were the new contours in my face. Gone was the puffiness and sagginess of civilized living. I'd already known I'd lost weight after having to cinch up my pants with a belt made from vines, but it became even more apparent when I saw my reflection. My face looked leaner. I liked it.

It occurred to me that, judging by the length of my hair, the beard growth, and the changes in my face, I'd been here longer than I'd thought. Although it felt like only a few days had passed since my arrival, the length of my hair seemed to indicate that it had been a month or more. The same could be said of my beard. Its scruffiness indicated that I'd been growing it for weeks, rather than days. Another indicator was the loss of fat and the addition of muscle throughout my body. I'd always been in fairly decent physical shape, but since arriving in the Lost Level, it had taken on more visible prominence.

I don't know how long I sat there, lost in my thoughts. I certainly wasn't paying attention to anything around me. It wasn't until the mournful call of an owl startled me from my musings that I remembered I was supposed to be on watch. I glanced at the fire and was surprised to see that it had burned down once more to just a few glowing embers. My gear was just beyond the fire, and Kasheena and Bloop lay past that. Had it been dark, they would have just been two dark lumps in the shadows.

The owl hooted again. I scanned the trees, looking for it. I didn't have to search for long. A large, winged form soared down from the treetops and perched on a low-hanging limb nearby. I studied the bird, and it did the same to me. As far as I could determine, it was a normal owl just like the ones we had back home. It turned its head slightly, staring at me with gold-rimmed eyes. I stared back at it, mesmerized. A sense of calm came over me. I relaxed. The owl's eyes seemed to grow bigger. I watched it, mesmerized. It didn't move. Just stared. And I did the same.

I was dimly aware of Kasheena stirring. She rose without a sound and crawled to my side, also staring at the owl. She didn't speak. She, too, seemed mesmerized.

The bird hooted a third time, and I tried to turn toward Kasheena, only to find that I couldn't move. The calm sensation vanished. Alarmed, I struggled against an unseen force that held me in place. I couldn't kick my legs out or move my arms, nor could I speak. Only my heart and lungs continued to work. The rest of me was paralyzed. I couldn't even swallow. The worst part was still having my wits, but being unable to do anything. It was frustrating to have my weapons within reach but unable to use them.

My alarm turned to sheer terror as the owl fluttered down from the tree limb and onto the ground in front of us. As I watched, the owl transformed, changing from a bird of prey into the pop culture representation of a grey alien. The entity's mass seemed to flow like liquid or twist like taffy as the transformation took place. The metamorphosis lasted only seconds. The alien was short, possessed a bulbous head and two large eyes, a small slit of a mouth, an almost non-existent nose, elongated arms, and disturbingly long fingers. The creature was dressed in a black one-piece uniform that ran from its feet up to its neck, leaving only its hands uncovered. The uniform had no discernible writing or markings on it—nothing to identify an affiliation or origin.

The alien regarded us with no visible emotion. A device appeared in its hand—a small, metallic rod with a blue-lighted tip, about the size of a stage magician's wand. The Grey pointed the device at us, and I felt a tingle go through my body, as if my limbs were numb and asleep. I tried to scream but to no avail. My body ignored my commands. I could barely breathe, let alone cry out. I tried tensing my muscles, desperate to break free, but nothing happened. Never had I felt so aware—or so utterly helpless.

A glowing sliver of light appeared behind the alien, some distance off into the forest and bright enough to stand out from the perpetual sunlight. I tried gritting my teeth, intent on breaking free, but nothing happened. The light quickly expanded into the shape of a doorway. Shadowy forms of other alien beings hovered in the doorway, watching the confrontation.

Our captor turned to face the door and began walking toward it. Inexplicably, Kasheena and I began to follow him. I fought with my body, desperate for control, but my legs continued to betray me. I caught a glimpse of Kasheena's face as she crossed into view. The terror and dread in her eyes mirrored my own. I struggled desperately to regain the use of my limbs, but I couldn't even grit my teeth, much less fight back. Hopeless and helpless, we were drawn toward the strange, looming doorway. The light grew brighter, so dazzlingly luminescent that it hurt my eyes. Its glare was strong enough to make me forget all about the ever-present sun for a moment.

I became aware of a low, monotonous hum. The noise was coming from the glow and seemed to vibrate through the entire forest, thrumming beneath our feet. Strangely, my ears popped, as if from a sudden pressure change, and my eyes began to water.

A second alien stepped out of the light and joined the other one. The two watched us, their expressions impassive, as we were drawn closer toward the strange glow. I tried one more time to break the inertia that held me captive, but it was useless. I was filled with despair. Had I been able to scream, I would have. Instead, I could only watch, feeling my terror grow with each step. The light became so bright that I could almost feel it on my skin. My vision grew blotchy, but still I was unable to turn away, or even blink.

Then, I heard a snarl behind us, and my heart jumped in elation. I recognized that growl. Had I been able to cheer, I would have done so loudly.

Seconds later, Bloop bounded forward, reacting savagely to the two aliens. Apparently, the strange force they'd used to spellbind Kasheena and myself had been ineffective on our bestial friend. Our captors seemed visibly startled, enough that the one holding the strange rod dropped the device. The blue light on the tip of the rod winked out. The creature bent, fumbling for it, and then Bloop was upon him—a furious, whirling, blue-furred cyclone of teeth and claws. He landed on the alien's back and wound his tail around his opponent's long, skinny neck. Then, with one quick, savage motion, his head darted forward, and he buried his snout in the Grey's throat, while slashing at its uniform and back with his talons. The alien uttered a pitiful, warbling cry—a shriek that was cut off seconds later as Bloop's jaws clenched shut in its neck. The alien gurgled. When Bloop opened his mouth again, there was a gaping, ragged hole where the victim's throat had been. Even as the creature toppled to the ground, Bloop leapt from its back and launched himself after the second alien, who turned and fled toward the light. I realized that Bloop wasn't carrying his swords. In his haste to save us, he'd apparently forgotten them.

With the death of our attacker and the apparent damaging of the mysterious rod from which it had controlled us, I found my paralysis was broken. I glanced at Kasheena and verified that she could move again, as well. She seemed disoriented, as if awaking from a troubling dream. I sympathized with her. I felt sluggish and tingly, as if I'd just awoken from a nap to find my hands and arms still asleep. I flexed my fingers and toes, trying to get the blood flow back to them, and called out to Bloop. My voice was barely a whisper. I paused, summoning my energy and trying to clear my head, and then shouted again, louder this time. Our companion ignored me, caught up in his single-minded pursuit.

The second alien ran toward the light, with Bloop hot on his trail. But as the duo approached the glow, the light quickly diminished and then blinked out altogether, reminding me of a television being switched off. The humming sound ceased as suddenly as it had begun. With a frightened yell, the Grey changed course, heading deeper into the forest. Bloop did the same, seemingly determined to mete out a punishment similar to the one he'd given its companion. Although the alien's language was gibberish to my ears, I could tell that it was frightened.

"Come on," I said to Kasheena, my voice hoarse and breathless. "We'd better go after Bloop. He's not armed."

"I would say that he is."

I shrugged. "Yeah, I guess you're right. Judging by the way he just killed that Grey, I suppose he doesn't even need those swords he's been carrying. But still...we don't know the full capabilities of his foe. It sounds panicked, and that makes it even more dangerous than before."

I quickly retrieved our weapons. Then, we jogged after our companion and his prey. Both of us stumbled a bit as we set off.

My limbs were still numb from the effects of the temporary paralysis but loosened up again as I ran. Bloop, suffering from no such malady, bounded ahead of us, crashing through the undergrowth like a bullet. I couldn't see the alien, but I did hear it, squealing with terror at being abandoned and pursued.

"Bloop," I called, cupping my hands around my mouth. "Come back!"

Ignoring my cries, our furry companion leaped onto a low-hanging tree limb and swung through the treetops, propelling himself along with both his arms and tail. Kasheena and I doubled our efforts to keep up with him, and our campsite faded from view. There was no way to get off a shot at our attacker and still keep pace.

We saw brief flashes of grey and black as the alien fled, darting among the thick vegetation. Overhead, branches shook and leaves cascaded down as Bloop raced along, moving even faster now that he was airborne. I soon found myself winded and gasping for breath. I noticed that Kasheena was panting, as well. I was just about to call a halt and suggest we give up when a horrifying shriek echoed through the forest, followed by a shout of surprise from Bloop.

Kasheena and I paused, glanced at each other, and then pressed on. The alien's screams increased, growing more frenzied and louder. Ahead, I saw Bloop drop down out of a tree. He recoiled fearfully from something I couldn't see. We raced toward him, weapons at the ready, but Bloop turned toward us and held out his hands, palms up, urging caution. Slowly, we approached, and what we saw made us both gasp aloud.

The Grey stood ankle-deep in a small puddle of water that was spread out along the forest floor. At least, it *looked* like a puddle of water. But it was doing things that water wasn't supposed to do, like flowing upward. As we watched, tendrils of fluid climbed up the alien's legs, entwining around the creature's body. More liquid followed, and then the entire puddle began to slide up, until the Grey was covered from the waist down. The alien thrashed and screamed but was unable to break away.

We backed up, watching in revulsion as our former attacker's body began to dissolve. The pain and terror reflected in those obsidian, full moon eyes was terrible to behold, and I felt my loathing for the Grey turn to pity as it slowly liquefied. The alien gave one last, anguished cry and then fell silent. Trembling, it continued to stare at us. Kasheena turned away from it, and I noticed that she was crying. Bloop grunted and then stared at the ground. I watched, unable to tear myself away from its gaze until the swirling water flowed over its head, extinguishing those orbs forever. Then, the elongated form splashed back to the ground, forming a puddle once more—albeit bigger than it had been before. The pool rippled and quivered and then went still.

I hadn't realized until that moment that I'd been holding my breath. A shudder ran through me as I exhaled, and that feeling of dread returned. I wondered how long could I realistically survive in a dimension where even the water could eat you. But then I glanced at my companions. I didn't know Bloop's origin, but Kasheena had been here all her life and was still alive despite that fact. At that thought, my fears eased somewhat.

Bloop motioned us backward, and we did as directed, creeping away in silence until the puddle was out of sight. Then, we turned around and retraced our steps back to the camp. As we walked, I touched Bloop's shoulder. His muscles were still taut and tense, but when he looked at me, he smiled.

"Thanks, buddy. You saved our lives tonight...today. Whatever it is here."

I stuck out my hand to shake. He glanced down at it, and then back up at me. His brow furrowed in confusion.

"I guess your people don't shake hands," I said. "And I don't know if you can understand me, but thanks. That's all I wanted to say. Just thanks."

He stared at me for a moment, and then his smile grew broader.

"Bloop," he said and pounded his chest with one fist.

I laughed, nodding. "Bloop, indeed, my friend. Bloop, indeed."

"What was that thing?" Kasheena asked. "It looked like water, but it...was not."

"I don't know," I answered, surprised. "I was just about to ask you the same thing. You've never seen something like that before?"

She shook her head. "Never. And I've never heard anyone in my village speak of such a thing, either."

"I noticed something during our journey. Every time we've stopped for water, Bloop has sniffed the source first. It didn't matter if it was a stream or a pool or even a puddle. He always smelled it first. I thought maybe he was checking to see if they were stagnant, even though that didn't make much sense at the time. But now I have to wonder if he was checking to see if the water sources were one of those creatures back there. Maybe he's had experience with them before?"

"Perhaps," Kasheena agreed.

"Maybe it was some sort of amoeba," I suggested. "Or some type of land-based jellyfish. Or a protoplasmic alien from elsewhere. It disguises itself as a puddle of water and then waits for its prey."

Kasheena said nothing, clearly still disturbed by what we had just witnessed. Bloop stood calmly against a tree. Using a twig, he cleaned alien flesh from beneath his claws. Then, he experimentally stuck the end of the twig in his mouth and tasted it. I assumed the alien's skin wasn't to his liking, judging by the face he made and the vigorous round of spitting that followed.

"Have you seen the aliens before?" I asked Kasheena.

"Aliens?"

"The things that tried to kidnap us. On my world, they're called Greys—although even there, most people don't believe in them."

"I have never seen one until tonight," Kasheena said. "But I have heard others speak of them before. It is said that they come from elsewhere, like yourself. They appear and disappear very quickly, and no one knows where they return to."

"But they live here, right?"

Kasheena frowned. "What do you mean, Aaron?"

"They live here in the Lost Level? They don't go back to where they came from before?"

"I do not know. I always assumed they must live here, as does everything else. Shameal suspected that they served the Creator, but in what capacity, he never said."

I thought about this while we hiked back to our campsite. The glow we'd seen had looked like some sort of portal, and when it vanished, so had the other aliens. The one who had been left behind—the one Bloop had pursued—had acted like it had been abandoned. Was it possible that the Greys had the ability to enter and leave this lost dimension at will? If so, then perhaps they were my ticket back home—if home was indeed where I wanted to return to. Before, I had thought so. But now...I wasn't so sure. This world was fraught with perils and hardships, but despite that, the thought of leaving made me a little sad.

As if reading my thoughts, Kasheena reached out, took my hand, and gave it a squeeze. She smiled. I returned the gesture.

No, I wasn't at all sure I wanted to return home anymore. And if I did, I wondered if she would be willing to return with me.

You might think, reading my accounting of the Greys, that I should have been more incredulous at the encounter, but you must remember that I'd long studied the occult and other esoteric mysteries. The Greys were a part of those studies—a small portion, to be sure, but something I'd read up on nevertheless. I had more trouble wrapping my brain around the giant robot and the mysterious sounds of underground machinery than I did alien abductors.

Something I *was* curious about though was Bloop. My thoughts returned to him once again, as they had right before we'd made camp. It felt like the more I learned about him, the less I knew. There was the matter of his apparent prior knowledge of that strange water creature, but I was also intrigued by his reaction to the Grey aliens. Although I couldn't be sure, I suspected that Bloop had encountered them previously, or at least had some sort of knowledge of their intent. I wondered if his people had legends of abduction phenomena just as my people had. It was also important to note that he had seemed immune to the paralysis they had induced on Kasheena and myself. How, and why? It frustrated me that I couldn't ask him. There was so much I wanted to learn, so many questions for which I felt he had the answers, but the communication barrier between us prevented me from getting those answers.

We made it back to the campsite without incident, but when I examined the ground, looking for the strange device the alien had dropped, I couldn't find it. Nor were there any markings on the ground where the weird light had appeared—certainly nothing indicating that a craft of some type had landed there. It was as if the aliens had never been there at all. Our own gear was unmolested, sitting right where we'd left it before the attempted abduction.

All three of us were still tired. Bloop let out several exaggerated yawns, and Kasheena and I both had circles under our eyes, but despite our exhaustion, none of us could sleep. After a half-hearted attempt at breakfast, we decided to move on and make camp elsewhere. Soon, we started off again, taking care to go far around the pool of killer water, but even after the campsite was far behind us, I kept glancing over my shoulder, looking for signs of pursuit. I don't know if it was nerves or paranoia or lack of sleep—or perhaps a combination of all three—but I couldn't shake the persistent feeling that we were being watched. But there were no more aliens or liquid blobs. Instead, the only thing I saw was that ever-present sun, hanging high over our heads like an unblinking eye.

Do you recognize anything? I Do you recognize Do you I Do anything? Do you recognize I Do I Do you recognize Do you recognize anything? you recognize anything? anything? Do you recognize I Do you I you recognize you anything? I Do you recognize you recognize I Do you recognize anything? Do you you anything? recognize anything? Do you recognize you recognize anything? Do you recognize anything? I Do you recognize Do you I Do anything? Do you recognize I Do I Do you recognize Do you recognize anything? you recognize anything? anything? Do you recognize anything? anything? Do you recognize I Do you I you recognize you anything? I Do you recognize you recognize I Do you recognize anything? Do you

9

S P E C I A L
D E L I V E R Y

"DO YOU RECOGNIZE ANYTHING?" I asked Kasheena after an extended, grueling hike up an especially steep and rocky hillside. I don't know how long our trek had worn on, but I was tired and thirsty, and my feet burned. I'd built up blisters during our journey to Kasheena's village, and our extensive climbing and walking had finally caused them to pop. The police riot armor had never seemed bulkier or heavier than it did at that moment. My throat and tongue felt like sandpaper. I applied some of John LeMay's cherry lip balm in the hope that it would make me salivate. I think Bloop was worn down, as well. His tail hung limp behind him, dragging the point of one of his swords through the dirt.

When Kasheena didn't answer me, I tried again. "Are there any landmarks that might indicate how close we are to your village?"

Nodding, she pointed ahead. "Beyond those trees lies the soft valley. As I told you before, I know that area well. Past the soft valley is a strange, small, yellow statue. After that, there is more forest. We should reach the shores of a lake before our next sleep. We will not linger there, for the waters are dark, and it is said that the lake is inhabited by a monstrous creature. My people have never seen this creature, but our elders have spoken of it. We do not fish there. Also, we have seen parties of Anunnaki along the lake's shore many times before."

"And your village is near the lake?"

"Not quite. After the lake, there are grasslands. It is perhaps another sleep before we encounter the Temple of the Slug, which we will also avoid. My village is only a short journey beyond that."

"What is it about this temple that makes you avoid it?"

"I do not know," Kasheena admitted. "My people are forbidden to go inside. It has always been this way. Those few who have dared to defy that rule, and have ventured into the temple, have never returned to tell what they found there."

I mulled it over. A soft valley. A yellow statue. A monster-haunted lake, perhaps with a bonus group of snake men patrolling its shores. And something called the Temple of the Slug. Before I could ask for more details, Kasheena turned away and pressed on. Bloop glanced at me, shrugged his furry shoulders, and followed after her. Sighing, I did the same.

"You seem distracted," I told Kasheena. "Is everything okay? Is there something you want to talk about?"

"I am fine," she said, even though she clearly wasn't, and it occurred to me that women were just as frustratingly similar and mysterious regardless of what planet, dimension, or alternate reality they came from. It had always been my experience that they wanted you to be sensitive to their feelings, but through clairvoyance, rather than communication.

I sighed again in frustration and followed along. When I glanced at Bloop, I swear it looked like he was grinning.

"Laugh it up, fuzzball." As soon as I said it, I remembered that Bloop had probably never seen *Star Wars* and therefore wouldn't understand the reference.

It occurred to me then that even if he had, we were still separated by our language barrier. It would have been easy to dismiss Bloop as an animal, or even a pet, but that simply wasn't true. Although we didn't know his origins, he was clearly from a bipedal race of creatures on an intellectual par, roughly, with humans. The fact that he could understand so much of what we communicated simply through studying our expressions, gestures, and tone demonstrated as much.

The ground began to slowly slope downward, and the trees thinned out, becoming shorter and more slender. Lush ferns grew in the rich, moist soil. Some of them had green fronds like back on Earth, but there were other colors, too—brilliantly hued oranges and reds and yellows. One of the ferns had leaves that looked quite similar to those of a marijuana plant. I wondered if it had the same influence when smoked. There were also wildflowers and other forest plants. Neither Kasheena nor Bloop showed any concern about them, so I assumed the foliage was safe.

Soon, our descent grew steeper. The trees disappeared completely, replaced with thick stands of shrubbery and undergrowth. Halting, Kasheena turned back to Bloop and myself.

"Watch your footing," she said. "There is a small game trail here, or at least there was the last time I traveled this way. It is not treacherous, but the soil is loose and rocky and can give way suddenly beneath your feet."

She took a few minutes to search the hillside and then uncovered the trail she'd mentioned, hidden between two large boulders. Kasheena started down the path, followed by Bloop and myself. It was steep and narrow, and the ground shifted beneath me several times, but after a short descent, the undergrowth cleared, and we reached the bottom. When we did, I simply stood and stared—incredulous.

"The soft valley," I muttered.

"Yes," Kasheena replied.

At first, I didn't comprehend what I was seeing. Oh, I understood it well enough. I could identify the strangeness of the items blanketing the valley floor. I just couldn't comprehend how such a thing was possible. Or *why*....

Back home, I'd done my laundry every Sunday afternoon at a laundromat around the corner on my block. I've always felt that there is nothing lonelier than doing laundry in such a place. Usually, I would take a book along with me to pass the time, but even then, I'd feel lonely and morose. Still, there was one part of that weekly ritual that always left me feeling slightly bemused, no matter how deep my depression. Every time I removed my clothes from the dryer and folded them on the table, I'd discover that one of my socks had gone missing. Never a complete pair. Always one lone sock. I'd check inside the dryer, under the table, and everywhere else for the escapee, but would never find it. I'd always wondered where those socks went.

Now, I knew.

Spread out in front of me as far as the eye could see were socks. Gym socks, dress socks, footy socks, children's and baby socks—every type and color you could imagine. They blanketed the valley floor from one side to another. Kasheena and Bloop waded into them, as if traipsing through a field of wheat. At their deepest point, the socks reached halfway up Kasheena's calves. Weeds jutted through in some sparse places, but most of the vegetation was buried beneath the pile. I noticed that none of the socks were in pairs. The assortment was mind-boggling—a myriad collection of colors and sizes and types.

"This…." I paused, unable to finish my sentence. Instead, I could only stare in astonishment.

Kasheena glanced over her shoulder. "Come along, Aaron."

Shaking my head, I followed after my companions. After a dozen or so steps, socks clung to the legs of my pants, and I heard small crackles of static electricity. It was having an effect on Bloop's fur, as well, which had puffed out, making him look like a freshly bathed cat who'd been sat under a blow-dryer. Socks clung to his bare legs and tail.

I wondered how long they'd been here—the socks. Some of them looked brand new. Others were obviously weather-beaten and worn. Were they like fallen leaves in a forest, with the top layer concealing older layers that had deteriorated into nothing?

"Hold on a second," I called out.

Kasheena and Bloop halted, turning back to watch me.

It occurred to me that my own socks were already worn through after all the hiking I'd done. They were also dirty and crusted from my popped blisters and sweat. I bent down and grabbed a few extra pair of socks, having no difficulty finding some that were my size. Then, I shoved them into my backpack. After that, I removed my boots. As neither Kasheena or Bloop were accustomed to wearing socks (at least as far as I'd seen), they seemed bemused as I went through the process. But I didn't care. I stared at my feet. My toes and heels poked through the holes in my dirty socks. I pulled my old socks free of my feet. They seemed stuck to my skin, and it felt wonderful to flex my bare toes. The comfort I felt after tossing them aside and putting on two pairs of new ones was almost sensual. I sighed, relishing the sensation. Indeed, it might have been one of the most luxuriant things I've ever experienced. I pulled my boots back on and stood up, feeling as if I could walk a hundred miles.

"Better?" Kasheena asked.

"Oh, yes." I nodded. "Like you wouldn't believe. Thanks."

"I am pleased."

"So am I."

A small breeze whistled through the valley, lifting a frayed dryer sheet and plastering it across Bloop's face. He brushed it away, grunting. The presence of the dryer sheet only confirmed my wild speculations. As bizarre as it seemed, this valley accounted for the missing socks back on my world—a phenomenon which most people had encountered at some point in their lives but had always laughed off. I wondered if it was possible for a person to wait here long enough, watching for a sock to appear, and if so, could one fling themselves through the dimensional doorway before it closed, materializing in a clothes dryer somewhere?

"Unbelievable," I muttered, and then laughed aloud at the image.

Kasheena turned around to face me. "Did you say something, Aaron?"

"Oh, it's nothing. I'm just...amused. Of all the things I've seen here so far, this is definitely the strangest."

But I was wrong. The valley of socks wasn't the strangest thing I'd seen in the Lost Level. What came after the valley was.

When we began hiking again, I felt reinvigorated. The blisters and aches didn't bother me nearly as much. The extra pair of socks I was wearing acted as a cushion. I walked in luxury.

We exited the valley and started across a wide, forested plain. The trees here were younger and smaller than those of the previous forest, and thick tangles of scrub grew between them, slowing our progress. Most of the vegetation was harmless, but I did spot a few patches of razor grass, and Bloop cautioned me with hand signals not to brush up against a particularly noxious-looking vine with waxy green leaves and thumbnail-sized thorns. Kasheena led us along the outskirts of the woodland until she found a narrow, winding game trail. We followed that into the trees. As we walked, I noticed again how quiet and standoffish Kasheena seemed to be.

"Are you sure there isn't something wrong?" I asked. "Have I done something to offend you in some way? If I have, I'm really sorry."

Sighing, she stopped walking. Bloop and I halted, as well. Bloop took advantage of the delay and urinated on a nearby tree stump.

"It's not you, Aaron." Kasheena stared at the ground, unable to meet my eyes. Her voice was a low, sad murmur. "It is my people. I am worried how some of them might react to you upon our arrival. And as we draw nearer to my home, that worry is growing."

"That's okay." I smiled. "I can make friends easy enough. I mean, I'm not an extrovert by any means, but I can be charming. I'm sure Shameal will like me, at the very least. We share similar interests, after all."

"It is not Shameal I am worried about. You are my suitor now. There are other men among my tribe who wished to fill that role. They may take umbrage to the fact that an outsider has lain with me. I am fearful as to how they might react. Some might wish you harm."

"I can handle myself, Kasheena. You really don't have to worry about me."

She put her hand on my cheek and stared into my eyes for a long moment.

"Yes," she said. "I know you can handle yourself. I just fear...the trouble it could cause, even if you are only defending yourself."

"Well, let's just cross that bridge when we come to it."

Kasheena frowned. "There are no bridges between here and my village. At least, not along the route we are taking. There is grassland and hills once we leave the forest."

Before I could explain, Bloop growled with impatience. Kasheena responded to his mood, and we moved on.

Soon, we entered a clearing. I noticed right away that the clearing was not a natural formation. The grass and trees had been cut in a straight line running through the forest. The weeds and scrub were barely ankle high, and the trees had been reduced to stumps. I wondered how often it was maintained and who was doing the landscaping. The formation was about the width of a one-lane road, and indeed, that's what it seemed to be, although it wasn't paved, nor was there any sign of wheel ruts in the ground.

"Someone made this," I said. "Where does this road go? Who built it?"

"I do not know where it leads," Kasheena replied, "but I have always been told it was built by the same ones who made the statue."

"The statue?"

"Yes." She pointed. "The one I mentioned earlier."

I let my gaze follow to where she was pointing. A shiny steel post stood several yards away, just on the far edge of the clearing. The post was about four feet high. Attached to the top of it was a metal, canary-yellow mailbox, complete with a little red flag to put up and down, indicating whether or not there was mail inside. Between this odd sight and the valley of socks, my incredulity finally reached the breaking point.

"You have got to be fucking kidding me."

Kasheena and Bloop were both puzzled by my outburst.

"It's a mailbox," I continued. "It's not a statue. It's a god-damned mailbox!"

"You sound agitated, Aaron."

"That's because I *am* agitated! It's a mailbox. It has no purpose here, and yet there it is. Somebody mounted it on that pole and stuck it in the ground along this pathway. Not to mention that somebody is cutting the grass here on a regular basis. So, who is responsible for all this? Because I'm fairly certain that the mailman or Globe Package Service aren't making deliveries here in the Lost Level."

"I don't understand." Kasheena's brow furrowed. "You are upset with me…."

"It's okay." I held up my hands in mock surrender and lowered my voice. I did my best to smile, but acid was churning in my stomach, and all I managed to do was grimace. "I'm not upset with you, Kasheena. Not at all. I'm just…I'm tired. I'm tired, and my head hurts. That's all. We've been walking for what feels like forever. I suggest we make camp here for a while. We don't have to sleep. I just want to rest a bit."

Kasheena nodded. "We will do so just beyond the tree line. It is not safe to camp out here in the open."

We made camp and ate a small meal and talked for a while, watching the sun hover motionlessly overhead. I yawned in mid-conversation and realized that despite what I'd said before, I needed to do more than rest. I needed sleep. Kasheena agreed that she could use some herself. We decided to take a nap and then continue on our way to her village. After a brief discussion, utilizing hand signals, we conveyed to Bloop that he should take watch and wake us when he was ready to renew the hike. Our furry companion agreed. I stripped off my armor and weapons, except for my dagger. Then, clad only in my underwear, jeans, and socks, I curled up next to Kasheena and promptly fell asleep, so exhausted that I was barely conscious enough to kiss her forehead before drifting off.

I dreamed of home, and like all dreams, it was a mish-mash of the mundane, the bizarre, and the insightful. In the dream, I was back in my old apartment, sitting on my bed, but the opening ritual hadn't worked, and there was no doorway into the Labyrinth hovering before me. I was sending text messages to everyone I knew, but I was typing them while pretending to be the character Mr. Darcy from Jane Austen's *Pride and Prejudice*. People were responding to me with confusion, but when I then told them it was me, they didn't respond at all. I sat there on my bed, wondering if I would have become a different man had I discovered Mr. Darcy before discovering Han Solo, and then decided that I was better off. Mr. Darcy couldn't make the Kessel Run in less than twelve parsecs. Suddenly, Bloop was there in the room with me, but he was wearing a baseball glove, a cowboy hat, and smoking a cigarette.

"You don't belong here anymore," he told me. His voice was a rich, deep baritone.

"You can speak," I gasped.

Bloop nodded. "Here, I can. But I don't like it. It's not natural."

Now I realized that we were no longer in my apartment. Instead, our surroundings had morphed into my childhood bedroom.

"You don't belong here," Bloop repeated, exhaling cigarette smoke. It curled around his head, forming halos that rose slowly to the ceiling.

"But this is my home. This is where I grew up. I lived here."

"Not anymore." Bloop shook his head, then walked over to my bookshelf and perused the volumes. "You're like me now. You don't belong here. Come home."

"I *am* home."

"No, Aaron. You're not. Neither am I. We can't go home again. We can never go back. They won't let us."

"Who won't let us? The Anunnaki?"

Bloop took another drag off his cigarette and shook his head. "No, the Anunnaki are trapped, just like we are. They can't go home, either."

"Then who are our captors?" I asked. "Who's preventing us from leaving the Lost Level? Is it the Greys?"

"Not exactly."

"Not exactly?"

"Not exactly," he repeated.

"Bloop, I don't understand."

"The Greys are but servants."

"Servants to who?"

My mother called up from downstairs, informing me that dinner was ready, but in the dream, she didn't sound like my mother. She sounded like my third grade teacher.

"It is time for us to go," Bloop said, but now the cowboy hat and baseball glove he'd been wearing were gone, replaced by a pair of round spectacles. Wearing them, Bloop looked a little bit more like the Marvel Comics character the Beast.

"Hang on," I replied, rising to my feet. "I want to tell my mom goodbye, at least."

"You won't be able to."

"Well, then I should pack some things first."

"You can't do that. You can only return with what you brought with you. They'll deliver everything else."

"I don't understand."

"Look at the moon." Bloop pointed at my window.

I moved over to it and parted the blinds. A full moon hung in the sky, whitish-yellow and seemingly swollen. As I watched the moon, it blinked. At first, I thought maybe it was me that had blinked, but when the moon did it again, I gaped.

"They are watching," Bloop said over my shoulder. "From the sun. And from the moon. They are always watching us. That's what they do. The sun and the moon are both eyes."

He placed his furry hand on my shoulder. I felt his claws against my skin, even through the fabric of my shirt.

The sensation increased as I woke to find Bloop shaking my shoulder, rousing me for my turn at watch.

"Buddy," I murmured. "You're just as exasperating in real life as you are in my dreams."

If Bloop understood me, he gave no indication. Instead, he knelt on his haunches, watching me until he was certain that I wouldn't fall back to sleep. Then, he curled up several feet away from Kasheena and closed his eyes. As it turned out, Bloop had been exhausted, too. His tail twitched a few times, and then he lay still, snoring softly.

I sat for a while, watching them sleep, and pondered the meaning of my dream. Unfortunately at the time, I couldn't make sense of it. It wasn't until many years later that I would understand the ramifications of it all.

Eventually, I pulled on my boots. Armed only with my dagger, I rose and padded away in search of some bushes to relieve myself behind. I had just finished and was zipping my pants, when I heard the distinct sound of hydraulics. They were quite similar to those of the robot we'd seen fighting the Tyrannosaurus, albeit quieter. Whatever the source of the noise, it was drawing closer. I perceived it to be coming from the nearby road.

I glanced back at my sleeping companions and then back toward the road. Deciding not to wake them, I crept through the undergrowth. If I saw any reason for alarm, I'd rush back and rouse them. I reached a tangle of vines within reaching distance of the mailbox and watched as another robot came into view. This one wasn't nearly as large as the one we'd seen fighting the dinosaur. It was about the size of a compact car and box-shaped. Its grey metal hull was splattered with mud and spots of rust. Spelled out on its side in large, stenciled, block letters were the words 'PROPERTY OF GLOBE PACKAGE SYSTEMS - USPDU 222-321-412' and some smaller lettering that I couldn't make out. A small, dinnerplate sized satellite dish rotated slowly atop the robot, nestled between two small poles that looked like lightning rods or antennae of some kind. The construct had no wheels or treads and hovered about twelve inches off the ground. Beneath it, I saw leaves and other debris blown to the sides of the road. Whatever the propulsion system, it was obviously pushing out air. That explained why the road appeared swept clear, as I'd noticed earlier.

The thing cruised along until it reached the yellow mailbox. Then, it slowed to a stop and hung motionless in the air. Flashing lights appeared on both its front and back. Inside its shell, I heard machinery running. As I watched, a small hatch opened in its side, and a mechanical arm popped out. The robot opened the mail-box, verified that there was nothing inside, and then the arm slipped back into the hull. Gears whined as the hatch closed again.

To this day, I still can't explain why I chose to do what I did next. As I sit here in this abandoned school bus, reflecting back on my time in the Lost Level and all of the things that have happened to me, my actions that night still perplex me. (I say night with irony, here in this land of perpetual day). I've made many mistakes during my life as an inter-dimensional castaway, and there are several of them that I wish I could take back, even though they seemed like the right thing to do at the time. But this one just confuses me. Maybe my actions were spurned by familiarity or curiosity. Maybe it was because, unlike our previous mechanical encounter, I could read the lettering on this robot's hull. It was something from my world, or a world similar to mine, albeit from the future. I recognized the name Globe Package Services, of course. If you're from my level, I'm sure you do, as well. In my time, they were the biggest package delivery company in the world and just one division of the massive Globe Corporation, an international conglomerate with so many subsidiaries and special interests that I doubt even the company's shareholders were aware of them all. Private security, computers, oil drilling, entertainment, fiber optics, medical technology and research, communications, publishing, food production, mining—they seemed to have a hand in everything, an infinitely-tentacled hydra of industry and finance. Some said they were too big. Indeed, in my time, there were conspiracy theorists who said that Globe secretly controlled the world—that they were the Illuminati and the New World Order all rolled into one. I wasn't sure about any of that, but judging by the robot, they had apparently taken over from the postal service at some point in the future.

Anyway, I don't know what compelled me to break cover and step out from behind my tangle of vines, but that's what I did. The robot remained where it was, hovering above the road. I took a few cautious steps toward the thing, wary of its reaction. I clutched my dagger in one hand, wishing too late that I'd brought another weapon from the camp. My pulse pounded in my throat as I waited to see what the robot would do.

"GREETINGS TO YOU, CITIZEN. NICE WEATHER WE ARE HAVING. IT IS ANOTHER SUNNY DAY."

Its voice was deep and booming and didn't sound at all mechanical. I was too stunned for a moment to speak and merely stood there gaping. Then, I cleared my throat and raised my hand in greeting.

"Hello."

I heard Bloop and Kasheena stirring behind me, roused from their sleep by the robot's voice. But before I could turn to look for them, the machine spoke again.

"WARNING. TAMPERING OR INTERFERING WITH A DESIGNATED POSTAL CARRIER IS A FEDERAL OF-FENSE, PUNISHABLE BY LAW. PLEASE LOWER YOUR WEAPON. FIRST NOTICE, AS REQUIRED BY STATUTE 81739."

"Lower my...?" Confused, I realized too late that the hand I'd raised in greeting was the hand holding the dagger. I quickly lowered my arm. "No, I'm sorry. I was just waving. I mean you no harm."

"THAT IS GOOD, CITIZEN. TAMPERING OR INTER-FERING WITH A DESIGNATED POSTAL CARRIER IS A FEDERAL OFFENSE, PUNISHABLE BY LAW."

"Yes, so you said. Listen...what are you, exactly?"

There was a brief pause, as if the robot was not sure how to answer the question and was calculating the best response.

"MY DESIGNATION IS GLOBE PACKAGE SERVICES UNITED STATES POSTAL DELIVERY UNIT 222-321-412. I AM TASKED WITH THE DELIVERY AND COLLECTION OF ALL INGOING AND OUTGOING MAIL ALONG THIS ROUTE."

I considered this. It was a bit surprising that, if the robot was from the future as I suspected, there was still physical mail delivery. It seemed only natural that in the future most mail would have been phased out in favor of electronic communications.

"Where are you from?" I asked. "And when?"

"THE SAN DIEGO HUB IS MY OPERATIONS CEN-TER, CITIZEN."

"San Diego? Can you return there?"

"NEGATIVE. MY NAVIGATION EQUIPMENT IS CURRENTLY MALFUNCTIONING. NORTH IS MISSING. MY NAVIGATION EQUIPMENT WILL NOT FUNCTION PROPERLY UNTIL NORTH RETURNS."

"North is...missing?"

"AFFIRMATIVE."

"So, you're stuck here, just like the rest of us."

"NEGATIVE, CITIZEN. I AM A GLOBE PACKAGE SERVICES UNITED STATES POSTAL DELIVERY…."

"You said that already," I interrupted. "If you can't find your hub, if you have no place to return to, then what are you doing here?"

"THIS IS MY DESIGNATED ROUTE. I AM TASKED WITH THE DELIVERY AND COLLECTION OF ALL IN-GOING AND OUTGOING MAIL ALONG THIS ROUTE."

Before I could respond, Bloop and Kasheena rushed up beside me. Bloop carried a sword in each hand, and Kasheena brandished one, as well, along with the handgun she'd recovered from the Anunnaki. I opened my mouth to warn them about the robot's aversion to weaponry, but the mail carrier beat me to it.

"WARNING, CITIZENS. TAMPERING OR INTERFERING WITH A DESIGNATED POSTAL CARRIER IS A FEDERAL OFFENSE, PUNISHABLE BY LAW. PLEASE LOWER YOUR WEAPONS. SECOND NOTICE, AS REQUIRED BY STATUTE 81739."

Bloop responded by growling. Kasheena held out the pistol, offering it to me, but I waved her away and turned back to the robot.

"CITIZEN, YOUR PET IS REQUIRED BY LAW TO BE LEASHED IN MY PRESENCE SO THAT IT DOES NOT INTERFERE WITH MY DUTIES. IF YOU HAVE ANY QUESTIONS CONCERNING THIS LAW, PLEASE REFERENCE REGULATIONS 7162353 AND 7162354 FOR MORE INFORMATION."

"Now, wait a minute," I said. "First of all, he's not my pet. He's an intelligent being, just like we are. And secondly, he doesn't mean you any harm. None of us do. They'll lower their weapons."

"I will do no such thing," Kasheena said, "until I know that this creature means us no harm in return."

"Bloop," our furry companion agreed, hefting both swords higher.

"WARNING. TAMPERING OR INTERFERING WITH A DESIGNATED POSTAL CARRIER IS A FEDERAL OFFENSE,

PUNISHABLE BY LAW. PLEASE LOWER YOUR WEAPONS. THIRD NOTICE HAS BEEN COMMUNICATED AND ACKNOWLEDGED, AS REQUIRED BY STATUTE 81739."

Kasheena frowned. "What does that mean?"

"NOW COMMENCING DEFENSIVE MANEUVERS," the robot replied. "PLEASE STAND BY."

Another hatch opened in the mail carrier's side, and three rods, composed of some type of flexible metal, emerged. They crackled with electricity, and the hairs on my arms and the back of my neck stood up. Bloop's fur did the same. He looked like he'd just tumbled out of a clothes dryer. His bangs and whiskers puffed in front of his eyes, momentarily blinding him. The robot swung the metal arms at all three of us. Kasheena and I managed to dodge. I ducked low, allowing the rod to sweep over my head, while she darted to the left and jumped behind a tree. Bloop, still unable to see, was not so lucky. The third rod touched his shoulder, and he screamed and jittered. I smelled burning hair. Continuous spasms rocked him, and the current jolting through his body made him unable to let go of the swords. Kasheena popped out from behind her cover and fired a shot, but there was no discernable reaction from our foe. I don't know if she missed or if its hull was just bulletproof.

The rod pulled away from Bloop, even as the other swung back around to strike at me again. I backpedaled out of range, furious at myself for only being armed with the dagger. I glanced around the ground, hoping to find a rock I could pelt the robot with, but before I could, the tips of the rods opened up, revealing pincer-like fingers. They seized Bloop—who had fallen to the ground, motionless, but still clutching both swords—by his shoulders and legs. Then they receded back to the robot. Clutching Bloop at its side, the mail carrier began to hover higher off the road.

"No!"

I rushed forward, dimly aware of Kasheena shouting at me, and leaped aboard the robot's roof just as it began to speed down the road. I had to hold my dagger between my teeth and grip the sides tightly to avoid falling off.

"WARNING," it said as we sped along, "TAMPERING OR INTERFERING WITH A DESIGNATED POSTAL CARRIER IS A FEDERAL OFFENSE, PUNISHABLE BY LAW.

YOU HAVE BEEN GIVEN THREE NOTICES, AS RE-QUIRED BY STATUTE 81739. DEFENSIVE MANEUVERS ARE COMPLETE. FURTHER OBSTRUCTION SHALL RE-SULT IN OFFENSIVE MEASURES."

I spoke through clenched teeth, enunciating slowly and desperately trying not to lose my only weapon. "I'm not trying to interfere with you, you goddamned bucket of bolts. Let my friend go, and we'll continue on our way."

"YOU CANNOT RECLAIM YOUR PET, CITIZEN. AS PER REGULATION 7162354, IT HAS BEEN DEEMED A DANGEROUS ANIMAL. YOU HAVE VIOLATED LEASH-ING LAWS. YOUR PET WILL BE EUTHANIZED UPON REACHING THE SAN DIEGO HUB."

"But you don't know where your hub is!"

"THERE MAY BE A BRIEF DELAY IN REACHING THE HUB UNTIL NORTH RETURNS. WE APOLOGIZE FOR ANY INCONVENIENCE."

"Then let my friend go!"

"NEGATIVE. YOU MAY MAKE ARRANGEMENTS TO SECURE HIS REMAINS ONCE THE EUTHANASIA PRO-CESS IS COMPLETED."

"The hell I will. I'm warning you, robot—"

"FAILURE TO FOLLOW COMMANDS REGARDING FURTHER OBSTRUCTION WILL RESULT IN THIS UNIT TAKING OFFENSIVE MEASURES. FINAL WARNING, AS PER STATUTE 81740. THIS UNIT APOLOGIZES FOR ANY INCONVENIENCE. PLEASE STAND BY."

Our speed increased, and the landscape began to flash past. I risked a glance behind us and was dismayed to discover that our campsite—and Kasheena—were already gone from sight. From my vantage point atop the robot, I could only see the top of Bloop's head and the tips of his ears. He remained in the unit's mechanical clutches, gripped tightly against the side of the hull and immobilized.

That was when I noticed a small, sealed access door about a foot away from me. It was similar to the hatch that had opened on the robot's side, but miniscule in comparison—about the size of a credit card. I wondered if I could pry it open with the dagger, but doing so would mean I'd only have one hand free to hang onto our speeding captor with, and we were traveling fast enough that I might fall off.

Seconds later, the robot made up my mind for me.

"NOW COMMENCING OFFENSIVE MEASURES. HAVE A NICE DAY."

The panel door opened, and a small nozzle, similar to that of a garden hose, rose out of the hatch. It swiveled toward me, and then spurted a stream of noxious, greenish-black fluid. Only my quick reflexes saved me. I ducked flat, cringing, and hugged myself against the robot's roof as the fluid arced overtop me and splattered a tree off to our right. I glanced over my shoulder and saw that the tree's trunk was smoking and liquefying. Whatever the strange fluid was, it was obviously highly corrosive.

As the nozzle readjusted itself, pointing lower to take aim at me again, I allowed survival instinct to override my paralyzing fear and let go with my right hand. There was a brief, terrifying second where I thought I might plunge off the back of the robot, but I readjusted my balance and squeezed so hard with my left hand that I felt metal biting into my flesh. With my right hand, I yanked the dagger from my mouth. The nozzle unleashed another stream, but I slid to the left, and it overshot me again. My relief vanished as a crosswind scattered a few tiny droplets on my legs. Immediately, my flesh began to sizzle. The pain was excruciating—like a bee sting full of battery acid. I was nauseated by the chemical smell of my own skin burning.

Screaming, I struggled to maintain my grip. I returned the dagger to my mouth again. Biting down on it helped me focus through the pain. I pushed myself forward and grabbed the nozzle before it could fire again. I was able to swivel it away from myself easily enough. Reassured that I had a good handhold, I let go of the robot's side with my left hand and retrieved the dagger once more. Then I jammed it into the hatch, driving the blade deep into circuitry and wires. I expected to be electrocuted for my efforts, but when that didn't happen, I stabbed the robot's innards again and again.

The pain in my legs was intense, and I suppose I momentarily blacked out—lost in some fugue state of panic, agony, and berserker rage. Eventually, I realized that my hair wasn't blowing in the wind behind me and that we had stopped. The robot was still hovering above the road, but it was no longer moving or speaking or trying to kill me. It had also released Bloop, who clambered atop the roof to help me. He sniffed at my legs and then recoiled. I pulled myself into a crouch and was just about to begin cutting the flesh away to try to stop the damage, when he leaped off the robot and scampered into the woods.

"Bloop," he called.

He bounded out of the trees clutching two great fistfuls of leaves. Using these, Bloop wiped the smoking corrosive from my skin, carefully making sure he didn't get any on himself. When he was finished, he tossed the leaves over the side and then inspected my wounds.

"Bloop," he said, nodding.

"Bloop, indeed," I responded. "Thanks, buddy."

The pain gradually subsided, and there was no further reaction. I stood experimentally and found that I was able to walk. After the wounds had clotted, Bloop helped me clamber down onto the road. The leaves he'd used to clean me were smoldering and blackened.

We inspected the robot. I'd been worried that it might recover and attack us again, or begin melting like the previous robot we'd encountered, but it did neither of these things. It was obviously still functioning. Hydraulics whined from somewhere deep inside its chassis. But it made no further move to attack us. Indeed, it didn't acknowledge us at all. Nor did it continue on its way. It simply remained where it was, floating above the ground.

"Come on." I clasped Bloop's shoulder. "The hell with this thing. Let's get back to camp. Kasheena is probably worried about us."

But as we soon learned, Kasheena had other things to worry about.

We limped along the road, Bloop recovering from his electrocution and subsequent paralysis and me wincing at the damage to my legs. I stared at the horizon, expecting to see Kasheena coming in search of us, but the road remained empty. A sense of uneasiness came over me and grew with each passing mile. Bloop must have sensed it, too, for he hurried his pace, and I had to struggle to keep up with him. When we saw the familiar yellow mailbox, we both broke into a run. I winced in pain but pushed my own discomfort to the side. There was still no sign of Kasheena, and I now desperately felt that something was wrong.

We found the first dead Anunnaki a few yards into the forest. The reptilian had been shot through the head. We found three more snake men scattered around our camp. All of them were dead. One's neck had been broken. The other two were shot. The clearing still reeked with their cucumber and mothball stench. It was clear enough what had happened. While Bloop and I had been gone, a group of Anunnaki had attacked the campsite. They had probably been watching us even before the mishap with the robot. I was certain that Kasheena would have pursued us, which meant that they had surprised her before she could leave. She had obviously killed all four. What was less obvious was her current whereabouts. She wasn't in the camp, and after a hurried search, we discovered that all of our gear and weapons were missing, as well.

I cupped my hands around my mouth and called for her. "Kasheena!"

The only responses were the startled cries of a few birds and the echoes of my voice. I looked around the camp for any signs of her—a scrap of her loincloth, perhaps torn in battle, or maybe a few strands of hair ripped out by a branch, or even a splash of blood, but there was nothing. Panicked, I left Bloop to continue scrutinizing our campsite while I searched in concentric circles in the area around it. I had visions of Kasheena lying somewhere beneath the trees, wounded or unconscious. I looped deeper and deeper into the forest, until Bloop summoned me back again with a cry.

"What is it?" I panted, out of breath. "Kasheena? Did you find some sign of her?"

Bloop was crouched down on his haunches, studying the ground around the campsite. He motioned me over, and I knelt beside him. He made sure that he had my attention, and then pointed at the dead reptilians. Then, he drew four lines in the dirt with the claw of his index finger.

"Four," I said.

"Bloop," he agreed.

He then drew nine more lines and swept his hand toward the forest. After a moment, I realized what he was trying to communicate. There had been thirteen attackers altogether. Kasheena had managed to kill four of them, but the other nine had captured her and stolen our gear. He pointed at the nine lines again and once more gestured into the forest. Then, he waved goodbye.

"Is she alive? Can you track them?"

I gestured with my hands, and he must have understood me, because he grunted urgently and pointed into the forest.

"Then, come on," I said, standing. "Let's go. They've already got a head start."

Snorting, Bloop beckoned at me to follow him.

"When we find them," I said as we plunged into the under-growth, "I intend to exterminate every single one of these moth-erfuckers once and for all."

"Bloop!"

"My sentiments exactly, buddy. Let's do this."

10

THE COWBOY'S TALE

BLOOP TOOK THE LEAD, TRACKING the Anunnaki through the forest. He did this partly by scent and partly by subtle signs on the ground—half a footprint here and a broken twig or bent leaf there. We made good time, despite our injuries and exhaustion. It helped that we were no longer burdened with equipment, armor, or weapons. Bloop had given me one of his swords, and I carried that, along with my dagger. He clutched the other in one hand, using it occasionally to hack at branches or vines or other impediments. I think he did this more out of frustration and restlessness than anything else. I felt the same way. I wished for my .45, but enraged as I was, I would have been just as willing to confront Kasheena's captors unarmed and tear them apart with my bare hands. At that moment, I was certain of my ability to do it.

We pressed on without stopping to rest, heedless of our physical condition. The forest was quiet. I took that to be a sign of the Anunnaki's recent passage, but I suppose it could have been from our presence, as well. Occasionally, Bloop would pause and listen for a moment or sniff the air. Then, he would bound ahead again. At times, I had to struggle to keep up with him. I grew frustrated with his speed. I'm certain he was equally frustrated with mine. Had I not been with him, he could have swung through the trees and made better time.

It is hard for me to say how far we ran. I estimate we'd gone at least two or three miles when we heard the gunshot—just a single blast and muffled by distance, but still unmistakable. That brought us both to a halt. We stood there, panting, and waited for the sound to be repeated, but no more shots were forthcoming. After a minute, Bloop started off again, and I followed, hoping he'd been able to determine which direction the shot had come from. I wondered what it had meant. Could Kasheena have managed to escape her captors and fired off a round with my pistol, or perhaps her own? It didn't seem likely. The Anunnaki would almost have certainly bound her as before, and I had to assume our weapons would have been safely stored on their person. My mind then turned to the possibility that it had been the snake men shooting at Kasheena, perhaps as she attempted to escape. There was also the possibility that the gunshot had nothing to do with her and was simply leading us astray.

Minutes ticked by. Maybe more than minutes. I was still musing over the origin of the pistol shot, however, when we stumbled across it for ourselves.

There was a man ahead of us with his back against a tree trunk and his legs sprawled out on the ground before him. He wore dirty, torn dungarees tucked into scuffed boots and the frayed remains of a shirt. His short brown hair was slick with sweat, and he was breathing heavy, mouth hanging open. He was obviously injured, with deep puncture marks all over his chest and abdomen, along with an even more grievous gash in his right forearm. Judging by the sheer number of wounds, I guessed his injuries to be fatal.

He didn't seem to be aware of us until we were almost upon him. When he finally saw us, the wounded man was visibly startled. I saw fear flash across his face, but he was obviously too weak to flee.

"My Lord," he gasped.

"It's okay," I said, stepping in front of Bloop. "We're not going to hurt you."

"Did..." He paused, shuddering as he drew breath. Blood trickled from the corner of his mouth. His accent marked him as not only an American, but a southerner. "Did y'all come through the canyon, too? Don't know how you...how you got past them things, but you'd better be careful. Their younger cousins are about."

"We came from that way." I pointed. "My name is Aaron Pace. This is my friend, Bloop."

"He ain't from around here," the man said. "Reckon I'm right about that."

"No," I replied. "None of us are."

The man tried to grin, but it looked more like a grimace. He licked his lips and then spoke again.

"You ain't hallucinations, are you?"

"No, friend. We're real enough."

"Figured as much. Can smell you both. Just thought maybe you might be, on account of your friend there."

"Sorry. And again, he may look scary, but I assure you, he means you no harm."

"Y'all got any water?"

I shook my head.

"Just my luck," he moaned. "I should have just let them lizards eat me when they got Terry and the Reverend back at the watering hole. At least then I'd have died in the water. Had me a last drink."

I knelt beside him and studied his wounds more closely. The punctures in his chest and stomach appeared to have been made by spears or pikes, but the two in his forearm were neater and more symmetrical, like a bite. The skin around those two holes was puffy and pale, and thin red lines ran out from the punctures, creeping up and down his arm.

"Snake bite," he muttered. "I would have beaten the sons of bitches if not for that."

My breath caught in my throat. "What kind of snake?"

"The kind that...walks on two legs. Big as a full-grown man. Never seen anything like them in my life. Course, I reckon that's been par for the course, last few days, what with the dead walking around eating folks and such."

I ignored this for a moment and focused on my more pressing concern. "This snake man? There was more than one?"

He nodded, then coughed. A bubble of blood burst from his lips.

"Did they have a girl with them?"

He nodded again, and my heart began to hammer.

"Yeah," he said. "They did. It was on account of her that I got bit in the first place. Bunch of them come marching through here just a bit ago. Had a girl with them."

"How many?"

"Just the one girl. Pretty little thing, but fierce, I reckon."

"No, how many snake men?"

"I make it nine. Took a shot at one, but I missed. I was down to my last bullet. Reckon if I'd had more, I could have killed them all real quick."

I looked up at Bloop, and he tilted his head, his expression quizzical. I nodded in affirmation and held up nine fingers. Then, I turned back to the injured man.

"Which way did they go?"

He tried to raise his hand and point, but then he groaned in pain and simply nodded instead.

"That way. I reckon you know the girl. Might ease your mind to know she didn't look hurt or nothing, least when I saw her. If anything, she looked mad enough to spit."

"That bite on your arm looks infected," I said. "I'm guessing poison."

"I reckon so. They got me during the fight. I got bit by a copperhead once, a long time ago, and it felt the same way. Except this might be worse. I reckon it has to be, on account of they left me alive. Why do that, unless they knew I was poisoned and would die anyway? Just wish I wasn't so thirsty."

"I'm sorry. I wish we had something for you to drink."

"That's okay, friend. And I don't figure either one of you for a doctor."

"We can't do anything for you," I admitted. "I'd tie a tourniquet around your arm, but I've nothing to use. And our friend, the girl that's with them..."

"I understand. She's still alive. I ain't, at least for much longer. But would you...could you stay with me until...?"

I hesitated. He was beyond our aid, and every moment we delayed meant Kasheena and the Anunnaki were farther away from us. The fact that they'd left him here to die slowly, rather than simply finishing him off indicated that they were moving quickly. If we lost their trail, we may never find her again. I couldn't leave her resigned to that fate. But the cowboy was dying and scared and alone. I remembered the fear I'd felt upon my arrival in the Lost Level, and then, against my better judgment, I agreed to stay. I simply did not have it in me to deny companionship to someone who was dying.

"Okay. We'll sit with you awhile."

He must have seen something in my expression or heard the regret in my voice.

"Don't worry," he said. "Like I said...I don't reckon it'll be much longer. I can feel that...stuff burning in my veins, getting closer...to my heart. If it don't get me, the spears they stuck between my ribs surely will. Pretty sure something's grinding together inside of me."

"No worries."

"Tell you what...if I take too long, y'all can finish me yourselves. Deal?"

Bloop grunted, impatient, and then swatted at a mosquito.

"Where are you from, friend?" I asked. "And what's your name? We'll do our best to leave a marker behind for you."

I had already decided not to ask him *when* he was from. Judging by the things he'd said so far, it didn't appear that the man knew the full extent of our circumstances or location, and I didn't see any sense in confusing him with explanations of time travel and inter-dimensional journeys.

"My name's Deke," he said. "I'm originally from a little town back in West Virginia, name of Brinkley Springs. But Hogan and I...Hogan's my partner...he and I come out here to Red Creek a little over a month ago. We'd pooled our money and bought quite a stand of timber. Planned on opening ourselves up a sawmill. But then that disease come along."

"Disease?" It occurred to me that perhaps Deke's coughing and wheezing had less to do with his wounds and more to do with some illness. I then became aware of just how closely I was crouched next to him.

"Hamelin's Revenge," he said. "You know? That disease from the Indian reservation back east?"

I shook my head.

"Well, if that don't beat all." Deke sighed, and more blood bubbled up from between his lips. "I must be farther from Red Creek and the canyon entrance than I thought. News travels slow out here."

"This disease," I gently prodded. "Is it contagious?"

"Only if you get bit by one of them dead things or get their blood or spit and such on you. Don't you worry none, Mister Pace. I ain't sick."

"Tell me more about this disease."

"Well...they say it started with rats. They overran an Indian reservation back east, but they weren't no ordinary rats. They were dead."

"You mean zombies?"

"I mean dead. But they still moved and bit like they were alive. They attacked the Indians, and those who got bit became sick and died. Then, just like the rats, they came back, too. And they came back hungry. Fella came straggling into Red Creek, sick from the disease. He told the town doctor all about it before he died. The Doc got some of the town bigwigs together, and while they were having a meeting about it in the back of his office, the dead man got back up and ate them. Then they came back, too. It spread through town, quick. The dead attacked the living—and not just dead people, either. No, sir. I saw dead horses, dogs, cats, coyotes and such."

Bloop grumbled, once more signaling his impatience and confusion over our delay. I motioned at him to be patient. I don't know if he understood me or not, but he wandered over to a nearby tree and relieved himself all over the base of the trunk. The pungent reek of urine was strong enough that both Deke and I winced.

"What is he?" Deke asked. "He like your pet or something?"

"He's a friend. I'm not sure what his origin is, or where he comes from, but I know that I can count on him."

"That's..." Deke broke off into a fit of coughing. I tried to sit him up, but he waved me away. When he was finished, he resumed talking.

"That's a good kind of friend to have. Hogan and me were like that. I didn't know any of the other folks in our party until we escaped town together. It was me, Hogan, Leppo, the Reverend, Jorge, Terry, and Janelle. We rode off into the desert...Leppo knew the terrain, so we were letting him lead us, but he died of heatstroke on the second day. By then, the dead had picked up our trail and started chasing after us. We got tired and thirsty, but they didn't. After a few days, they caught up to us. We rode for some hills, trying to escape a flock of dead birds. What we found was a canyon...I'll never forget that, to be sure. The mouth of it looked just like an archway. It was the damnedest thing. Almost like somebody had made it.... We headed in and come out in the middle of a huge valley that seemed much bigger than the canyon itself. The terrain was different, too. Instead of desert or scrubland, it was a forest. And not forests like they got out here in this part of the country. No, sir. Hogan said it reminded him of the ones back in Virginia.... At first I thought it might all be a mirage, but even the air smelled different, and the trees were real enough to touch. We didn't...think too much of it at the time, on account of we found that watering hole I mentioned earlier."

Bloop wandered back over to us and crouched on his haunches. Deke stared at him for a moment, clearly uneasy, but then he relaxed and continued. I noticed that his voice was getting weaker.

"So, we're in this oasis...and there's a stream running along the valley floor. We headed on down to the watering hole, and everything was fine until they showed up."

"The dead?"

Deke shook his head. "The lizards. Not like them snake men...these were different. Hogan said men of science call them...dinosaurs. I reckon you've seen them around."

I nodded, noticing as I did that the blood flow from the wound in his arm had slowed to a trickle.

"There was four of them...ambushed us. Killed the horses and then moved on to Terry and the Reverend. That was when...the dead showed up. Coyotes...infected with Hamelin's Revenge. They must have...followed us from the desert into the canyon. They...fought with the dinosaurs, and the lizards ate them. We got away and huddled up for the night. In the morning...we tried to find our way back to the canyon mouth, but my compass wasn't working. Damned thing...just spun round and round, like it couldn't find north. We headed out on foot...trying to find our way back...and then..."

He broke off again in a fit of coughing, spraying blood all over himself. I pulled away, making sure none of it had landed on me. When he leaned back against the tree again, his breathing was harsh and ragged.

"Dead dinosaur found us...ate Jorge...me and Hogan and...Janelle climbed the ridge...figured we were lost.... Hogan said we weren't where we were supposed to be...another time...back before there were humans...said the disease must be what killed off the dinosaurs.... I didn't...believe...went looking for the archway...found another one...looked like a door...ended up here...couldn't find...way back...."

He stopped breathing, and I was sure he was dead. Blood flowed from his mouth and nose. Then, suddenly, he gasped, arms flailing weakly.

"Hogan and Janelle still back there...in the other place.... Somebody got to find them.... I ain't infected...no dead here...just want to go home...find the door...home.... I...the door back...."

His breath hitched in his chest. He shuddered once and then lay still, eyes open and staring at nothing. This time, I was sure he was dead.

Bloop staggered to his feet and said, "Bloop."

I picked up two leaves. Using them to protect my fingertips, I reached out and closed Deke's eyes, holding them shut with my fingers until they stayed that way. Then I glanced up at my companion.

"I know you're anxious to go. I am, too. But there's something we need to do first. I don't know how much you understand of what I say, but this is important. We can't just leave him lying out to rot. First of all, he deserves better than that, and I promised him. Secondly, the place where he came from—there was a disease. He might be infected with it. He might not. But if he is, we can't risk it getting loose here in the Lost Level."

Bloop grunted softly, inferring some understanding from my

tone if not my words. He watched as I grasped the hilt of my sword with both hands and pressed the tip of the blade against Deke's forehead. Grimacing, I pressed with all my might, driving the sword through his skull and brain until I felt it strike the tree trunk behind him. The sounds this elicited were gruesome. Trying to ignore them, I wrenched the sword free. The blade was covered in gore. Deke's corpse slumped to one side. Using leaves, I cleaned the blade as best I could, being careful not to get any of his blood on me.

"There," I panted. "If he is infected, according to everything I've always heard about zombies, then that should keep him from coming back. Now, give me a hand."

Moving as quickly as possible, I stretched Deke out flat on the ground and then began to fashion a cairn overtop his corpse with rocks and tree limbs. The Anunnaki had stripped him of his belongings, except for his tattered, bloodstained clothing. Bloop watched me for a moment, and then, realizing what I was doing, began to assist me. Between the two of us, we'd soon completed a decent burial. It wouldn't protect him from a hungry Tyrannosaurus, but I was confident our efforts would deter smaller predators and scavengers. It would have to suffice, in any case. I hurriedly scratched his first name onto one of the rocks, and then I nodded at Bloop.

"Let's go."

"Bloop!"

We started off into the forest again in pursuit of Kasheena and her reptilian captors. It was slow going at first, until Bloop picked up their trail once more, and then we increased our speed. The brief rest we'd had while delayed by Deke had been beneficial, as we both seemed to have renewed stores of energy. My injuries from the fight with the robot still pained me, but they were more manageable now.

I ran on autopilot, trusting Bloop's tracking abilities, and mulled over everything Deke had told us. His story fascinated me. Obviously, he'd come from not only an alternate reality, but from the past—a level where a zombie apocalypse had occurred during the days of the Old West. At some point, he and his party had wandered out of that reality and into another. He'd mentioned a rock formation that had reminded him of a doorway. A passage into the Labyrinth, most likely, but the question was where had that doorway taken them? Deke had mistakenly thought he was still in that place when Bloop and I had first found him. He'd described it as forested and populated with dinosaurs, so it was reasonable to assume that it had looked similar to the landscape here in the Lost Level. But then, at some point, he had discovered yet another doorway and gone through that alone, presumably arriving here.

My mind swam with the myriad possibilities this presented. If the zombies had followed Deke from his time to the time of the dinosaurs, could they have also followed him from there into the Lost Level? If so, what did that mean for all of us here? If there was supposedly no escape from the Lost Level, and it was a closed ecosystem, then the effect a virus such as a zombie plague would have on this environment was too terrible to consider. Every living thing here would eventually be decimated.

The thought reminded me of what I'd read in my occult studies about the Siqqusim, Elilum, and Teraphim—three races of entities led by creatures named Ob, Ab, and Api. All three groups moved from planet to planet, level to level, working in waves and completely exterminating every living thing until nothing was left. Then, after reducing that planet to a cinder, they moved on to the next world. Luckily, all three races had been confined to a realm known as the Void for millennia. But the damage they could do if they were ever freed was remarkably similar to what something like a zombie virus could do to a self-contained ecosystem like the Lost Level. I shuddered, hoping that my preparations during Deke's makeshift burial had been enough and that nothing else infected had followed him here.

It occurred to me that, although our time together had been brief, I hadn't asked Deke for the location of the doorway which had led him from that primordial world to here. The thought had never even crossed my mind. My concerns were focused solely on rescuing Kasheena, rather than any effort to return home. Of course, even if I'd known where to find Deke's second doorway, there was no guarantee it would still be there, nor would stepping into an alternate-reality infested with undead dinosaurs be a more preferable alternative to the world I currently inhabited.

Life in the Lost Level was terrifying and difficult, but I could tolerate the dangers and discomfort as long as Kasheena was with me. It was time to get her back, and I vowed to myself that once we'd rescued her, I would never be far from her side again.

Had I only known then what I know now.

11
SLAUGHTER ON THE SHORELINE

EVENTUALLY, WE HEARD THE SOUND of rushing water ahead of us and to the left. The Anunnaki's trail must have gone in the same direction as the noise, because that was where Bloop led us. We emerged on the banks of a wide, fast-moving stream. The water appeared to be fairly deep. Bloop didn't pause to sniff it, so I assumed it was normal water and not something like that strange amoeba we'd encountered before. In the middle of the stream, I saw the occasional ring left behind by fish striking at insects on the surface. A small brown snake slithered away from us, clearly frightened. Clouds of mosquitos and gnats hovered around us, buzzing incessantly, but I barely noticed. The vegetation thinned along the rocky banks, allowing us to increase our speed. We ran downstream, still moving single-file. Bloop paused less often, seemingly certain now of which direction Kasheena and her captors had gone.

Further proof that we were on the right trail occurred when we found the dead Anunnaki. The snake man lay partially on the stream bank with his legs in the water. It was clear from the position of his head that someone had broken the creature's neck. The corpse's armor, weapons, and gear were still attached, and its scaly skin, although cool, was still pliant and soft to the touch. Clearly, its death had been recent. It had only been armed with a short spear and a club. I left the weapons where they were, preferring my sword and dagger.

Scattered footprints in the creek mud added to the tale. One set, obviously belonging to Kasheena, headed off into the forest. Other tracks, belonging to her captors, clustered around the dead snake man before following her into the woods. I surmised that she had somehow managed to kill one of the Anunnaki and break free long enough to escape. The others had gone after her. Whether she had been recaptured or was still on the loose remained to be seen.

We were about to start off after her when a new sound rang out—the clang of steel clashing against steel. This was followed by a gunshot. While Kasheena's trail led to our right, away from the water, the noise of battle was coming from further down-stream. Bloop and I glanced at each other, and I pointed ahead of us. We ran toward the sounds, and after a short distance, emerged onto the shore of a vast, mist-enshrouded lake. The shoreline was thick with boulders, ferns, and reeds, and the water gently lapped at our feet, but we barely noticed it, gaping instead at the battle taking place a few hundred yards away from us.

We had journeyed hard, consumed with saving the princess, but as it turned out, Kasheena didn't need saving after all. Clutch-ing a sword with both hands, she stood facing four snake men. Four others lay dead, scattered along the shore. Anunnaki blood dripped from her blade, glistening in the sunlight. More gore was splattered across the rocks and running in rivulets from the corps-es into the water. Her shoulders and breasts heaved as she took a deep breath, and the fury in her eyes was both terrible and beauti-ful to behold. Two of her attackers were armed with stone-tipped spears. A third had a handgun. I recognized the weapon as the .45 I'd found in John LeMay's Jeep. The fourth snake man was un-armed. The latter ducked low, trying to charge her from the side, but Kasheena pivoted out of its way and let the creature charge past her. Amidst the confusion, she slashed at the Anunnaki armed with the pistol, severing its hand at the wrist. Both the weapon and the hand that had been holding it fell to the ground. The wounded snake man hissed, tongue protruding grotesquely, but otherwise made no sound. I had time to wonder if they screamed telepathically, as well.

"Hey," I shouted, "how about we even the odds a bit?"

"Bloop!" my furry companion agreed.

The unarmed Anunnaki and one of the spear carriers turned in our direction. The third jabbed his weapon at Kasheena, aiming the jagged point at her abdomen. She deflected the attack with her sword and then kicked the snake man in the stomach, knocking the offender backward.

I grinned. "Serves him right for stealing my gun."

Snarling, Bloop charged forward. I did the same, bellowing my own battle cry and hoping to distract and disorient them just a moment longer. My plan worked. Kasheena took advantage of the confusion and skewered her opponent, thrusting her sword through his chest until the tip of the blade protruded from the creature's back. Then, before Bloop or I could reach her, she'd lopped the head off the unarmed Anunnaki.

The lone surviving Reptilian turned tail and fled, running straight for the water. Kasheena gave pursuit, and Bloop and I changed course, trying to head it off. It beat us to the water and plunged into the surf with a tremendous splash. The snake man waded out a few yards and then abruptly stopped. Waves crashed against its waist as it stood there, trembling. Instead of facing us, it stared at something in the swirling mists.

"No mercy," Kasheena yelled. "The lake will turn red with its blood!"

Realizing there was something wrong, I skidded to a halt and tried to grab Bloop's arm. I realized that at some point during the battle he'd recovered another sword and was now armed with two of them again. Growling, he yanked away from me. Both he and Kasheena continued running toward the lake. The snake man continued to tremble in place, seemingly paying no attention to us.

"Kasheena," I shouted. "The waves…."

Just moments before, the water's surface had been calm, with only small currents gently lapping at the shore. Now, it was turbulent and churning with foam, as something rose from the depths further out from shore. With a great splash, the massive form breached the surface, and Kasheena and Bloop halted. The Anunnaki dropped its spear into the water, gaping at this new terror.

The creature looked like a cross between a crab, a lobster, and a scorpion, but it was nearly the size of a full-grown elephant. Two black, beady eyes glared at us from atop reed-like stalks on its head. The monster was armed with two serrated pincers. Each of the claws were nearly six feet in length, and tinted with a red and magenta crisscross pattern, which deepened to black at the razored tips. Additional smaller legs stuck out from beneath its carapace. I noticed that its long tail was equipped with a bulbous stinger. As it surged forward, propelling its monstrous bulk through the surf, the beast's claws rasped together, making a terrible racket.

CLICK-CLICK...CLICK-CLICK....

More of the creature's body emerged from the lake. It reared up on its segmented back legs and swayed back and forth, studying us. Water streamed off its blood-red shell. The monster emitted a warbling sort of hiss from its beak-like mouth and then rushed forward, splashing toward the terrified Anunnaki. The serpent man turned away. Maybe he meant to retrieve his spear, or perhaps he'd simply intended to flee. Whatever the case, the lake monster was faster. It caught the snake man just as he reached the shoreline. Looming over its prey, the creature plunged that horrific stinger into the Anunnaki's back. We watched in revulsion as the tail pulsed and throbbed, pumping some type of venom into the hapless victim. The Anunnaki thrashed helplessly, writhing in pain. His lidless, serpentine eyes rolled back into his head.

The monster clacked its claws together again, making that deafening *CLICK-CLICK...CLICK-CLICK....* sound. Its eye-tipped stalks tracked Kasheena as she hurried over to where Bloop and I stood, but the creature didn't pursue us. Instead, the beast kept its prey pinned on the shore, pumping more venom into his thrashing form.

I heard a hissing sound. Seconds later, the Anunnaki's scaly skin began to bubble and blister as if he were being microwaved from the inside. The snake man screamed soundlessly as the pustules swelled and then burst. Thrashing in agony, the Anunnaki's forked tongue lolled as it vomited a grisly mix of blood, bile, and steaming chunks of what appeared to be its own dissolving internal organs.

"My God," I whispered. "He's melting."

The wind shifted as the Anunnaki vomited again. The stench was atrocious, and my eyes watered.

Bloop closed his eyes and turned away from the horror.

Kasheena clutched my shoulder. "We should go, Aaron. It is still distracted."

I nodded, but made no effort to follow. Instead, I merely gaped as the beast yanked its tail free from the victim's back. Gore stained the creature's stinger. The Anunnaki's squirming grew weaker and spasmodic, and then ceased altogether. The snake man's flesh smoked and sizzled, sloughing from his bones in a wet, soupy mess as the acidic venom continued to liquefy his body. Using its claws, the lake monster shoveled the glistening, still-steaming pool into its mouth with greedy, slurping sounds.

"Aaron," Kasheena repeated, her tone more insistent. "Bloop. We need to flee! Come along."

The monster stopped feeding at the sound of her voice and turned its attention back to us. Hissing, it slowly clambered over the rocks and waded further onto shore. I quickly surmised that despite its ponderous bulk, it was fast and calculated that we would be in reach of that deadly stinger and those snapping claws before we could hope to escape.

Bloop must have reached the same conclusion. With a savage roar, he brandished both swords and charged headlong at our attacker. He swung one of the weapons in a powerful arc, but the monster seized the blade in one claw and ripped it from Bloop's grasp. Steel buckled and bent as it squeezed the sword. It tossed the useless weapon aside and jabbed at Bloop with its tail, but Bloop dodged the attack and slid beneath the behemoth, slashing at its insect-like legs. It seemed to have no effect on the beast.

I ran over to the corpses of the Anunnaki that Kasheena had killed and grabbed the fallen pistol, still clutched in one severed reptilian hand. Freeing the weapon, I turned back to face the monster. Bloop was no longer in sight, lost somewhere beneath its underside. Kasheena had moved to the creature's right side and was jabbing at it with her sword. Each time it scuttled toward her, she backed up out of striking distance of its stinger and claws. The beast raised its pincers and clacked them together in frustration.

CLICK-CLICK...CLICK-CLICK....

"Kasheena," I shouted. "Stay back!"

Standing with my feet shoulder-width apart, I extended my arms, took aim at the creature's neck, and squeezed the trigger. The gun kicked in my hands, and my aim was true, but the bullet, like Bloop's sword, had no effect on the armor-like carapace. The monster turned to face me, hissed, and then clicked its claws together again.

CLICK-CLICK...CLICK-CLICK.....

I lined up my second shot, aiming this time for its mouth, but when I squeezed the trigger, the pistol clicked. I pulled the trigger four more times in rapid succession, but the gun was empty.

Cursing the Anunnaki, I tossed the pistol aside and moved to recover my sword as the monster charged me.

"Aaron," Kasheena screamed. "Run!"

I did just that, seizing the hilt and scurrying backward, unable to take my eyes off the doom rushing toward me. I held my sword out in front of me as if to ward the creature away, but I had little doubt it would do any good. It was like trying to fight a tank with a toothpick. The beast swiped at me with one giant claw, attempting to knock me off my feet, but I managed to avoid the blow. Seconds later, I accomplished the task for myself by tripping over a large stone jutting up from the mud behind me. I fell to the ground, and my sword slipped from my hands and clattered on the rocks. I lay there sprawled on my back as the crab-thing reared above me. A bead of noxious-looking venom dripped from the tip of its stinger. Its pincers clacked together with a maddening racket.

CLICK-CLICK...CLICK-CLICK...CLICK-CLICK...CLICK-CLICK....

I shuddered, expecting that terrible cacophony to be the last sound I ever heard.

Suddenly, the creature flailed, waving its claws as if in pain. It shrieked—a high-pitched, liquid sort of sound that made me wince. As it reared up higher on its back legs, I saw the source of its obvious distress. Bloop clung to the underside of the monster's belly, using his hands and feet to hold tight. His tail wielded his remaining sword, which was buried up to the hilt in a groove between the shells protecting the beast's abdomen. Bloop sawed the blade back and forth, working it deeper into the soft tissue. Black blood welled around the sword handle, and when Bloop yanked it free, the trickle became a gush.

Furious, the crab-thing dropped to the ground, trying to crush Bloop beneath its bulk. As it did, Kasheena jumped onto a boulder and then leaped atop its back. She wobbled unsteadily, desperately trying to maintain her balance on the slippery carapace as our foe thrashed and shook. Then, she sat astride it, wrapping her legs around its neck as best she could and swiping at the antennae-like eye stalks with her sword. Unlike the rest of the creature, this part of its anatomy wasn't armored. The sword cleaved the appendages like a scythe cutting wheat. The effect was instantaneous. The beast screamed, a sound so loathsome and horrid that to this day, I still occasionally hear it in my sleep. Its frenzied and violent thrashing increased. Kasheena struggled to hang on, but the monster shook her off, throwing her as a wild bronco tosses its rider. She landed nearby, close enough to be trampled beneath its feet should it turn toward her.

Unable to tell if she was conscious or not, I screamed her name. There was no response. I grabbed my sword and sprang to my feet. As I ran toward her, I heard a cracking sound from beneath the creature. The beast gave one last squeal and then toppled to the ground—dead.

I ran to Kasheena's side, shouting her name, certain that she was dead. My relief was overwhelming when she sat up and pushed me aside, assuring me that she was okay.

"Bloop?" she asked. "Did he—?"

From beneath the creature, we heard a muffled response. "Bloop...."

"He's alive," I said. "Hurry. Let's get this thing off him."

The two of us placed our hands beneath the creature's carapace and tried to lift it with all our might, but the dead thing wouldn't budge. We tried again, panting and straining until the tendons stood out in our necks and shoulders. Still, we couldn't move the carcass.

"Bloop," Kasheena called. "Can you hear us? Are you okay?"

There was no response.

"We need a wedge," I gasped, wiping the sweat from my brow with the back of my hand. "The tree line. Help me find a limb we can use!"

We started toward the forest, but before we'd gone three steps, we heard a cracking sound behind us. I turned, apprehensive, expecting to find the monster moving again, and indeed, it was. However, the movements were tiny, a quivering that seemed to come from the center of its mass. That was also where the noises were emanating from.

"Inside," Kasheena whispered. "A parasite, perhaps?"

I nodded, envisioning a monstrous tapeworm bursting from the thing's back, or perhaps a brood of young hatchlings erupting from their dead mother. The carapace began to splinter and crack. Kasheena and I stepped back, weapons at the ready. The hole widened, and a moment later, the tip of a sword blade poked through the carapace. The hole grew larger still, and something furry and covered in gore thrust its head from the wound. It was our companion, so matted with the creature's innards that we didn't recognize him until he spoke.

"Bloop."

Kasheena and I rushed to the carcass while Bloop struggled to free himself. He spat and sputtered, grunting as he managed to squeeze more of his bulk through the crack in the shell. The stench wafting from inside the creature was horrific, and unfortunately, Bloop stank of it, as well. Every inch of his body was slick with gore, and his fur, normally full-bodied and luxuriant, was now greasy and stiff and pressed flat against his body. He glistened in the sunlight, wet and sticky and reeking like a slaughterhouse. Laughing, we helped him free. I'm sure all three of us were a terrible sight. Bloop plunged into the water and bathed himself as best he could, shaking like a dog when he was done. Kasheena and I washed the gore from our hands and then cleaned our wounds.

When we'd finished, I suggested we leave the area with some haste, lest another lake monster emerge. The others agreed with me. We gathered what weapons and gear we could. We were unable to find and recover any of the items they'd taken from our campsite, but we did find Kasheena's pistol. In the end, we were each armed with a sword. Plus, I had my dagger, and Kasheena had her handgun, which contained three unfired rounds.

Exhausted, we limped into the forest, retracing our steps. I risked one glance back at the lake, but its surface was calm. Already, a few scavenger birds circled the creature's carcass from high above. I wondered how long it would take them to strip the flesh from the lake monster and the Anunnaki, and felt a great sense of relief when the lake faded from view.

"We are not far from my village," Kasheena promised. "The worst is behind us now."

"I hope you're right."

"I am."

But she was wrong.

So, tell me what happened? So, tell me happened? what happened? So, tell me tell me tell me what So, tell me what happened? So, me So, tell me So, tell me what happened? happened? tell me what what happened? So, tell me what happened? me what what what happened? So, what happened? tell me what happened? So, tell me tell me tell me what happened? So, what happened? So, tell me what happened? So, tell me happened? what happened? So, tell me tell me tell me what So, tell me what happened? So, me So, tell me So, tell me what happened? happened? tell me what what happened? So, tell me what happened? me what what what

12.

THE
OCTOPHANT

"SO, TELL ME WHAT HAPPENED?" I asked Kasheena as we renewed our hike. "How did they manage to capture you again?"

"When you and Bloop were carried away by that...what did you call them? Robots?"

I nodded.

"I ran after you," she continued, "but the robot moved too quickly. I could not keep up with it. I tried calling out to you, but by then you were too far away. So, I returned to our camp, intent on stowing our gear, arming myself, and then rescuing you both. But before I could do so, the Anunnaki ambushed me. They had been lying in wait. I don't know how long they were tracking and spying on us, but they must have decided to take advantage of our separation. I fought back, but their numbers were too many."

"You managed to kill several of them," I said. "Don't be too hard on yourself. That was pretty impressive."

"Bah!" Glowering, Kasheena pushed aside a low-hanging branch and spat. "I should have been able to kill them all. And had I not been preoccupied with rescuing the two of you, I would have."

When she saw me grinning, she stopped walking. Her frown increased, and when she spoke again, there was a distinct edge to her voice.

"You find this amusing, Aaron?"

"Not at all." I held up my hands in mock surrender. "I just think you're remarkable."

"How so?"

"Just...here you are, a beautiful princess. According to the stories on my world, I should be the one rescuing you from danger. But clearly, you don't need any help in that regard. If anything, it's you who's been keeping me safe all this time. Bloop and I both owe you, Kasheena. You are a remarkable woman."

"Are the women of Earth not warriors, as well?"

"Oh, they are," I admitted. "But it took our society a long time to see them as such. Too long, in my opinion."

"What did your women do, if not fight?"

"Well, for a long time, women didn't have the same rights as men. They were viewed as second class citizens. Do you understand what I mean by that?"

"They were deemed not as important as the men."

"Right. We pretty much only saw women as caretakers. They were supposed to raise our children, cook our meals, and keep the house looking clean. Those attitudes passed in time, at least in most of our society. But even with those attitudes gone, and even after women made great strides in equality, we still managed to sexualize them before considering any of their other attributes. Even our warrior women had a sexual component to them."

"All living beings require sex," she said. "It is natural to notice the sexuality of another."

"Yeah, but this was different. Sex shouldn't be the first thing you notice about a woman."

"You say I am beautiful and pleasing to your eyes. Was that not the first thing you noticed about me?"

I shrugged. "It was, but only because we hadn't spoken yet. I hadn't gotten a chance to know you—the person you are inside."

"Then, I do not see why it is considered wrong that you noticed your physical attraction to me first."

"Well, there are a lot of people back on Earth who would disagree with you."

She was quiet for a moment. Then she said, "Yours is a strange world, Aaron Pace. The more you tell me of it, the more I am certain that I would not want to visit there. I am puzzled that you miss it."

"The longer I stay here, the less I miss it," I admitted, smiling. "Although I could do without things like the tikka-birds and the Anunnaki."

Kasheena returned my smile. "As could I."

She led us onward. My injured leg pained me somewhat, but I was able to keep pace with the others. I noticed that Bloop seemed to be moving somewhat slower, as well. He didn't seem lethargic or less agile. Just...tired. We all were.

We'd gone perhaps another mile or two when we came across an area where the treetops were thin. Vast, dense undergrowth filled this part of the forest, but the shrubs, weeds, and smaller trees had recently been trampled underfoot. Judging by the scope of the devastation, whatever had passed this way had been large in size.

Bloop soon discovered a series of footprints among the tramped down vegetation and motioned for us to come look at them. Crouched on his haunches, he hooted softly. I assumed he knew what type of animal they belonged to, judging by his behavior. I had no such luxury. Despite all those years spent hunting and exploring Minnesota's woodlands, I'd never seen footprints like these. They were a distinct reminder of my situation. Each track was roughly the size of a dinner plate and had four large, stubby toes. I saw no sign that the toes were equipped with talons or claws, but given the depth of the impressions, the creature had to weigh a considerable sum. It must have had an equally impressive stride, given the distance and spacing between each imprint.

"Do you have any idea what type of animal made these?" I asked Kasheena.

She shrugged and shook her head. "No, but I think Bloop might."

"Yeah, I had that impression, too."

Bloop turned to look at us, pointed at the tracks, and said, "Bloop!"

"Is it dangerous?" I asked, hoping he'd understand my intent, if not my actual words.

"Bloop." His tone was affirmative.

"We must be cautious," Kasheena whispered as we started our trek again. "Whatever this creature is, those tracks are fresh. It could still be about."

As we pressed forward, the forest slowly receded, giving way to a woodland that wasn't so densely packed with trees and undergrowth. This landscape, in turn, changed into a series of rolling, grass-covered hills with only a few trees growing upon each.

"These are the grasslands I spoke of," Kasheena said. "We are very near my home."

I felt a vague sense of unease, but couldn't determine why. A light breeze brushed over my skin, cooling my sweat. I glanced up at the sky, but all seemed normal. It was blue and cloudless, and the sun remained stationary. A few birds flew overhead, and a family of Slukicks chattered from a nearby treetop.

I turned my attention to the grasslands spread out before us. The blades were thick like cornstalks and reached far over our heads, bending slightly at the top. They swayed gently in the breeze, making a soft rustling sound.

"This grass isn't the kind that attacks people, is it?"

Kasheena laughed. "No, Aaron. It is just grass."

"That's good."

"It is the things that hide within the grass that attack people. So, we must be on our guard."

Approximately one-hundred yards to our right was a swath of grass that had been flattened. It reminded me of the pictures of crop circles from back home, but rather than taking on an elaborate geometric shape, the path of crushed grass merely led forward in a seemingly straight line. The swath was perhaps a little wider than an automobile. When we investigated it closer, we saw a few more of the odd footprints in various places where the beast had crushed the stalks into the dirt. There were also two massive piles of droppings, and the spoor looked and smelled fresh. Only a few insects flitted about them, indicating to me that the feces hadn't been there long.

"What do we do?" I asked.

"We follow the path," Kasheena said. "It will make our passage that much easier. We are nearing the Temple of the Slug, and my village is beyond that. With this path, we will save much time."

"I'm not so sure about this."

"You have misgivings, Aaron?"

"Yes, I do. I understand we're close to your home, and I'm sympathetic to the fact that you want to hurry, but consider this. If there are more Anunnaki on our trail—and we have to believe there are, given their previous tenacity—then this tall grass makes for a perfect ambush. They could be waiting in there, and we'd never know it until it was too late."

"Which is why we should follow the path," Kasheena insist-ed. "It is broad enough for all three of us to walk side-by-side. It will be harder for the Anunnaki to surprise us."

She strode into the field, following the trail of crushed grass. Bloop loped along beside her. After a moment, I reluctantly hur-ried to join them. We ventured deeper into the grassland, up and down the small, rocky hills. The terrain was treacherous. Craggy stones jutted from the dirt and rodent-holes dotted the hillsides, both providing plenty of half-hidden obstacles to stumble over. The vegetation grew so high that it was impossible to see anything on either side of us, even from atop higher ground. I considered climbing one of the sparse, stunted trees in an effort to survey our surroundings, but Kasheena vetoed that idea.

"The sap of those trees is unpleasant," she warned. "You see how no birds or other creatures nest within their limbs? That is because the sap causes your skin to burn and blister. A grove of trees like these grows near my village. My people sometimes use the sap to coat our weapons before battle."

"Is it enough to kill a person?" I asked.

"No, but it is enough to make one wish they were dead. The burns are very painful and the blisters never heal well. They leave scars."

I eyed the trees warily. "Thanks for the warning."

"Of course. I like your face and hands the way they are, Aaron. They are pleasing to me. I would not want to see them disfigured."

"Neither would I."

We'd continued on, following the path through the grass for a while longer, when we heard a terrible sound—a loud, baritone moan of anguish, followed by another. We stopped where we were, listening fearfully, and a third cry came. Whatever was mak-ing that awful sound seemed to be directly ahead of us, concealed just over a hilltop. I glanced at my companions, but could tell by their expressions that the noise was just as alien to them as it was to me. Crouching on all fours, I began to crawl forward, sinking low enough to the ground that my stomach scraped against the rocks. Bloop and Kasheena did the same, and together, we crept up the hill. Upon reaching the top, we heard a ponderous, labored panting from below. We slowly peered over the side and our eyes grew wide. Beside me, Kasheena gasped.

"Bloop," Bloop whispered. His tone was reverent.

At the bottom of the hill, lying amidst a circle of crushed grass, was a female creature the size of an elephant. Indeed, at first glance I thought it was an elephant, as she bore the same hide, colorings, ears, tail, and bulk of the elephants back home. But she differed in one shockingly distinct way from anything familiar on Earth. Instead of one singular trunk, the beast had a cluster of eight hairy trunk-like tentacles surrounding its mouth. They weren't lined with suckers, the way an octopus' or squid's tentacles were. Instead, they simply seemed to be additional trunks, each one capable of performing individual tasks. My breath caught in my throat as I realized what I was looking at— the fabled octophant of occult legend, a creature consigned to the same catalogue as unicorns, griffins, dragons, and other mythical beasts. Yet here it was, a fairy tale made flesh.

And she was making flesh of her own, as well.

The octophant let out another great bellow of anguish and convulsed. At first, I couldn't figure out what was causing her such distress. Her teats looked painfully swollen, but that didn't seem to be enough to cause such a commotion. Then, with a start, I realized that she was giving birth. The grass around her was wet with fluid, and she was extremely dilated. As we watched, another shudder ran through her great grey bulk.

"What can we do?" I whispered. "How can we help her?"

"We do not," Kasheena replied. "This is part of nature. It happens every day, and without humans around to aid the process. The only thing we must do is be mindful not to disturb her."

I nodded in agreement, and then glanced at Bloop. He seemed to understand, as well.

We clustered together, watching in amazement for the next twenty minutes or so, while the octophant gave birth. I longed for the binoculars the Anunnaki had stolen from us. At one point, my eyes grew blurry, and I discovered that I'd been crying without even knowing it. When I saw gummy fluid streaking the fur on Bloop's face, I realized that he was crying, as well. My heart went out to the beast. I wanted so desperately to help her as she struggled, but I knew that Kasheena was right. That didn't make it any easier, though.

Eventually, with one tremendous final push and a cry that echoed across the field, the mother octophant delivered her baby onto the wet grass. It was pink and grey and glistened in the sun-light. Panting, the mother cleared the newborn's face and multiple trunks so that it could breathe, and then nuzzled the infant gently. Kasheena, Bloop, and I clasped at one another in joy and wonder as the newborn squealed.

We watched for a few minutes longer, enraptured by the sight as the mother used her tentacle-trunks and tongue to finish clean-ing the baby. The newborn mewled and cooed, and my heart pounded at the sound. It tried to crawl away, testing its legs, but the mother was having none of that. When she pulled it close and the infant began to nurse, Kasheena tapped Bloop and I on the shoulder and motioned for us to follow her. We did, cautiously creeping backward so as not to disturb the creatures. When we'd reached a safe distance away, and were concealed once again in the high grass off the path, we stood smiling at one another.

"That was incredible," I breathed. "I've never seen anything like it."

"It was indeed wonderful," Kasheena agreed. "I must tell my father of it when we reach my village."

Bloop grunted at us both, and then crouched, brushing the grass away to expose a patch of soil. After ensuring that he had our attention, he used one of his talons to draw a crude series of figures in the dirt. Two of them were obviously the mother and baby octophants. The third was also an octophant, but much big-ger than the other two, and possessing tusks in addition to the eight tentacles. I understood his meaning right away.

"The daddy octophant," I said. "Of course. We should prob-ably head out of here."

"But we did not see a mate," Kasheena said.

"No, but Bloop seems to have some experience with these animals. If he thinks the father is lurking around, then we should make ourselves scarce. The last thing we want is a creature that size mistaking us for a threat to his family."

"Very well," Kasheena said. "We will—"

Something whistled through the air, and Bloop roared in pain. He clutched his left thigh. I glanced down and saw an arrow shaft protruding from it. More arrows rained down upon us, em-bedding themselves in the dirt or snapping against the rocks.

"Get down," I shouted, pulling my sword.

Then the smell reached us—that now all-too-familiar reptilian odor that signaled the arrival of the Anunnaki.

Kasheena had readied her weapon, as well. She crouched above Bloop, scanning the high grass for movement, while he rolled around on the ground in pain. He'd drawn his injured leg up and was grasping feebly at the arrow shaft with blood-slicked fingers. I crawled over to them and grabbed his furry wrist.

"No." I shook my head. "Don't pull it out. Not yet. We need to get you somewhere safer first."

Growling, Bloop bared his fangs at me. I drew my hand away, afraid he would bite me, and he reached for the arrow again. This time, I restrained him more forcefully.

"No, Bloop. If you pull that out now you could bleed to death! Just stay down."

He gritted his teeth, but made no move to attack me. Instead, he whined in pain. The grass rustled around us.

"On your feet, Aaron," Kasheena said. "Something is coming!"

I jumped up and stood with my back to hers.

"Here." She handed me her pistol. "I prefer both hands to wield my sword."

Nodding, I quickly checked the chambers. I wasn't familiar with the model or the caliber, and the weapon's markings were in a strange language that I didn't recognize, but I saw there were three bullets left. I gripped the gun in one hand and my sword in the other. The reptile smell grew stronger. It seemed to be coming from all around us.

Bloop thrashed in the grass, obviously agonized and in shock. The sight filled me with rage. The air felt charged, like before a thunderstorm. My pulse pounded in my ears.

Kasheena and I moved together in a slow circle. All around us there was movement as something rushed toward us through the grass. Seconds later, the vegetation parted and nine Anunnaki emerged and attacked. Two of them were armed with bows and lingered behind the rest. The others displayed an assortment of weapons—axes and swords and knives. I was grateful to see no firearms among this group, and even more grateful that I had one.

They attacked as a group, rushing us all at once. The archers remained behind, perhaps not wanting to risk shooting one of their companions. The Anunnaki closest to me charged with his axe held high, ready to bury it in my head. Before he could do so, I extended my arm and shot him point blank in the face. The snake man flopped backward, dying as he'd attacked—silently. I parried a sword thrust with my own and simultaneously fired another shot at a third attacker, but my aim was off and I missed. I saw a head go flying into the grass, trailing blood and tendons, and assumed that Kasheena had been responsible for the decapitation. I heard her grunting and cursing behind me, but was too engaged with the battle to turn and see for myself.

I dodged another sword thrust and returned one of my own, slashing my attacker's side, but in doing so, revealed my unguarded ribs to another opponent. The Reptilian thrust at me with his knife, but at the last moment, was jerked violently off his scaled feet by Bloop, who, despite his injury, had managed to loop his tail around the creature's legs and trip him. I turned my attention back to my primary foe, while Bloop ripped the fallen Anunnaki's throat apart with his talons. The snake man jittered helplessly as he bled out onto the ground. An arrow whizzed by me, close enough that I felt the wind of its passage. Kasheena dropped the archer who had fired it. I hoped it was the one who had shot Bloop.

We parried and struck and fought, but soon, our attackers had pressed us together with Bloop beneath our feet. I raised the pistol and squeezed the trigger and was aghast when my last remaining bullet misfired. Now, I was out of ammunition. I dropped the useless weapon to the ground and gripped my sword with both hands. The snake men paused, as if communicating to one another, and then tensed, ready to charge. I had no doubt we'd be unable to withstand their onslaught.

Just then, there was a terrible trumpeting noise, and the ground trembled beneath our feet as something crashed toward us. The grass parted, and the male octophant towered over us all, eyes blazing with fury. Its tusks were as long as javelins and thick as telephone poles, and its writhing tentacle-trunks looked strong enough to crush a steel safe like it was nothing more than an aluminum can. We stood paralyzed with fear, as did our attackers, as the enraged father lumbered toward us, bellowing a horrifying cry. He grasped one Reptilian with a trunk and began to squeeze, while simultaneously knocking aside another with a brush of his tusk. The stunned Anunnaki could only lay there, clawing at the ground as the octophant trampled him under one foot, pulping the snake man into red and green jelly and splattering the rest of us with gore. The sounds this made were terrible. The other helpless victim, still clutched in the beast's trunk, wriggled helplessly. The octophant smashed him against the ground, repeatedly, splintering the snake man's bones. Then, the monster tossed the limp form aside and glared at the rest of us.

I was hesitant to attack the beast if I could at all help it. After all, the father was just protecting its mate and offspring. Unfortunately, I could tell by its stance that the octophant would give no quarter. It intended to slaughter every living thing in our cluster. I briefly wondered if there was any hope of temporarily joining forces with the loathsome Anunnaki and defending ourselves together, but before I could devise a way to communicate this to them, the octophant charged again.

The serpent men scattered as the beast plowed toward us. I pushed Kasheena out of the way and then hurriedly helped Bloop to his feet. The octophant blundered between us, spearing an Anunnaki through the chest with his tusk while snatching another one with a serpentine tentacle. The impaled Reptilian slid down the tusk, staining it with gore. Its hapless companion struggled as one of the trunks squeezed his midsection. His eyes bulged, and his forked tongue protruded. Blood erupted from his mouth and nostrils.

While the octophant's back was to us, I dragged a whimpering Bloop into the grass and found Kasheena. With our injured companion supported between us, we retreated through the vegetation, doing our best to not only stay concealed, but get as far away as we could as quickly as possible. Bloop made a valiant effort to remain quiet, but I could tell he was in agony. His fur was matted with pungent sweat, and he'd bitten through his lip to keep from crying out. Blood oozed around the shaft protruding from his thigh, and already the limb was swelling. He was wobbly on his feet, but remained upright with our help and seemed determined to press on, despite recently being crushed beneath a giant crab-lobster-scorpion monster and then shot in the leg by an arrow.

Behind us, the sounds of the octophant's violent rampage continued. I kept glancing over my shoulder, certain that it would pursue us at any moment, but it seemed to be occupied with the remaining Anunnaki. I wondered where this particular group had come from and how they'd discovered us. Were they related to the other patrols we'd encountered, or had our paths crossed simply by chance? It occurred to me that if the creatures communicated telepathically, which all evidence seemed to indicate, then it was possible that one of the previous groups we'd killed might have sent out a call for reinforcements to any other Anunnaki within the area. How far did their telepathy reach? More importantly, where was their base camp or main civilization? They had plagued us at nearly every step throughout our journey, despite our long trek and the different regions we'd travelled through. I wondered just how large their numbers were and once again found myself pondering the possible reasons they had for so diligently attempting to capture us. They'd shown no hesitation to kill us, when directly threatened with the same, but it was clear that they'd prefer to take us alive. But for what purpose?

I was still mulling over these questions when I became aware that Bloop had gone limp. Panicked, I called a halt and laid him down in the grass between us. After checking his pulse, I was relieved to discover that he was not dead, but merely unconscious. His breathing had grown shallow and hitched, and his lips were pulled back from his teeth, revealing gums that had gone from black to grey.

"We've got to get this shaft out of him," I whispered. "Is there any chance the Anunnaki could have poisoned the arrow?"

"It is doubtful," Kasheena said, stroking Bloop's fur. "They prefer their captives alive."

"That's what I was thinking, too. He's probably just gone into shock. But no matter how badly they might want us alive, if we don't help him soon, Bloop's going to die."

"I do not believe the octophant will follow us."

I nodded, noticing how quiet the grasslands had become again. "It's probably gone back to its mate. But even so, I'd still like to put some more distance between us."

"We cannot drag Bloop between us in this state."

"No," I agreed. "We can't. I'll carry him. You'll have to take point."

Kasheena frowned in confusion. "Take...point?"

"Take the lead," I explained. "I'm going to have my arms full with Bloop, so you'll have to lead the way, watch for dangers, and protect us if something attacks."

"So, you wish me to do what I have been doing all along?"

It took me a moment to see that Kasheena was joking.

"Well played," I laughed. "Yes, exactly what you've been doing all along."

She leaned over Bloop and gave me a quick kiss. Her lips were soft and warm, and even in that fleeting moment, she took my breath away. Then she stood up, readied her sword, and beckoned at me to follow—all business.

"Wait just one minute," I said.

I cut a large strip of cloth from the bottom leg of my jeans and used it to make a tourniquet above Bloop's injury. He groaned, but remained unconscious. As gently as possible, I scooped him up and draped him over my shoulders, holding fast to his arms and legs so that he wouldn't slip off. I stooped over, struggling to remain upright and balance his weight. Walking while carrying him took a great amount of effort and concentration, but I managed.

Kasheena led us down a hill into a narrow, dry creek bed. The grass grew even higher along its banks, concealing us completely. We followed the gulch, and walking became easier. I still struggled with Bloop's weight, however. I felt like I was carrying bags of cement. My shoulders ached, and my arms and leg muscles began to burn. The grasslands remained quiet, and there were no further signs of pursuit from either the octophant or the Anunnaki. Gnats and mosquitos buzzed incessantly around my face and ears. Unable to swat them away, I could only grit my teeth in annoyance and keep plodding along.

"Perhaps we should remove the arrow here?" Kasheena suggested.

"No," I said. "We're still too close to the octophant's lair, and I don't relish the idea of that daddy stumbling across us while we're in the middle of working on Bloop. Plus, these aren't the most sanitary of conditions. Isn't there a structure or some form of shelter nearby?"

"There may be, but the only place I know of for certain is the Temple of the Slug, and it would be foolish to venture inside those walls."

"But why? If it's a walled-compound with a roof, then it would offer us protection and give Bloop a chance to rest. What's so forbidden about this place? Why do your people fear it so?"

"I have told you before that I do not know, Aaron. Ever since I was a child, I have been warned of venturing into the temple. We will have to find another place. Come. Let us continue. We will find something else. I am sure of it."

"How can you be so sure?"

"I did not know this creek bed was here. There is no telling what else might be hidden beneath the grass."

"That's what I'm afraid of."

Kasheena didn't reply. She stalked forward, staying alert. After a moment's hesitation, I followed her.

Bloop moaned, still unconscious.

"Hang in there, buddy," I whispered. "We'll find a place to take care of you soon."

And then we did, and even considering the strangeness of all I had experienced, the Lost Level surprised me again.

. 13 .
GHOSTS OF THE
FOURTH REICH

FATIGUE BEGAN TO GNAW AT me as we followed the gulch. I struggled with Bloop's weight. Desperate as I was to get him to safety and take care of his leg, I still needed to stop and rest. I was just about to tell Kasheena this when we came across the flying saucer.

That in itself wasn't so surprising, especially given our previous encounter with the Greys. No, the strangeness came from the markings on the side of the craft—multiple renditions of a symbol that clearly indicated the UFO had originated on Earth. Perhaps not my Earth, but an Earth all the same.

The craft was relatively small, roughly the size of a sedan, but disc-shaped. It was manufactured out of some sort of heavy, silver metal that I couldn't immediately identify. Sunlight should have glinted off the surface, but instead, the object seemed to swallow all light. Its shape reminded me of Saturn— a sphere surrounded by a disc. One edge of this outer disc was embedded deep into the terrain, and dirt and rocks lay piled up around it. Judging by the vegetation growing around it, I guessed that it had crashed here long ago. There was no obvious damage to the ship—no cracks or ruptures or signs of fire. There were also no windows or hatches. The outer hull was entirely smooth, with no visible means of entry into the craft's interior. There were no visible marking, either.

Except for the swastikas.

"What is it?" Kasheena whispered.

"A flying saucer."

Kneeling, I laid Bloop in the grass. He stirred, but did not awaken.

"A flying—"

"It's like the airplanes we found. People used it to travel through the air."

"Your people?"

"No," I said, eyeing the swastikas. "Definitely not my people."

"Is it safe?"

I shrugged. "It looks like it's been here awhile. See how the grass and vines are growing over it? I'd guess whoever flew it here is long gone. And that's good."

"They were bad people?"

"Yes." I nodded. "They were very bad people. Worse than the Anunnaki."

We set to work on caring for Bloop. I built a small fire while Kasheena searched for water. It took me a long time and a lot of frustrated curses to manage doing so. I wished for a lighter, or some of the fire stones we'd had earlier, but had to resort to striking my dagger and sword together to produce sparks. The entire time I did it, I worried that the noise of steel on steel might attract predators, but none came. By the time Kasheena returned, I had the fire going hot. I'd used dry grass and fallen tree limbs for tinder, and was dismayed by how much smoke the grass produced, but there was nothing we could do. Kasheena eyed the billowing smoke apprehensively, and I could tell she was troubled by it, as well.

"It's not great," I admitted, "but I'm just glad I could get it going at all. I wish we had some fire rocks."

"They are rare in this area," she replied.

"Yeah, I remember you saying that before."

"I found a small spring of good water nearby. But I do not think this fire is a good idea. If there are other Anunnaki about, they will see this."

"I know," I admitted, "but we need hot water in order to do this. Also, I'm convinced that they have the ability to track us through other means. Sight, hearing, and smell, of course, but given their telepathic abilities, I have to wonder if they've been able to find us via extrasensory abilities. Perhaps they've been tracking us via our thoughts."

Frowning, Kasheena placed the water over the fire. She'd found some type of brown gourd out amongst the grass and had used that to carry the water in.

"Think about it," I continued. "Different groups of Anunnaki have come upon us at different times throughout our journey. Now, I could accept that in one or two instances they stumbled across us due to blind luck. But for it to happen so often? That suggests to me that they were hunting us specifically. And given how determined their attacks have been, I have to assume revenge is now a part of it. We don't know what their original intent was when they captured you and Bloop and your uncle, but it's beyond that now. They want blood. Vengeance. Somehow, word of each group we've slain has made it back to the larger community. If they can do that, then it stands to reason they can track us through similar means."

"You sound worried, Aaron. Do not be. You have said yourself, we have bested them with each attack."

"Yes, we have. But if they are following us, what happens when we reach your village? We could end up leading them there."

"The Anunnaki have been a thorn in my tribe's side since before I was born. We do not fear them. It would not be the first time they have encountered our village. My people would slaughter any who dared set foot there. We always have before."

Before I could respond, the water began to boil over, and I turned my attention back to the grisly task at hand.

"He's unconscious," I told Kasheena, "but I need you to hold him down anyway, in case he wakes up while I'm doing this."

Nodding, she sat her weapons aside and knelt over Bloop. She straddled him, putting her knees on top of his shoulders, and then leaned forward, grasping his wrists. Bloop didn't move. Satisfied that she had his upper body restrained, I sat across his legs, readjusting the tourniquet to make sure it was tight. Then, I slowly worked the shaft out of the wound. Bloop moaned and twitched, but his eyes remained shut. His tail slowly coiled. I blinked the sweat from my eyes and continued, cursing in frustration. The arrow's barbed tip was caught in his flesh. Pulling my dagger from the fire, I used the heated blade to dig the arrowhead free.

The moment I touched the hot metal to his flesh, Bloop howled with pain. His eyes shot open, and his tail lashed out, swatting me in the face.

"Hold him," I shouted. "You've got to keep him still."

Grunting, Kasheena doubled her efforts, putting all her weight on his struggling form. His tail lashed out again, curling around my wrist. I wrenched it free with a gasp.

"Bloop," I cried, "it's us! Calm down, buddy. It's going to be okay."

Bloop roared, resisting with all his might.

"Damn it, Bloop. It's me. It's Aaron and Kasheena. Let us help you!"

He growled in response, thrashing and clawing at the dirt. Then, with a great shudder, he passed out again. I returned the blade to the wound, wincing at the smell of burning fur and flesh. The arrowhead was free within seconds, but it seemed like an eternity. I inspected the shaft, making sure there were no broken pieces still hidden inside his flesh. Then, I tossed the arrow aside and examined the wound. It was a ragged hole, about the size of a quarter. Blood leaked from it despite the tourniquet, and there were already signs of infection. I cleaned it as best I could, using all of the water we'd boiled. Then, I bound and bandaged it and sat back on my haunches, wiping the sweat from my brow. Kasheena climbed off Bloop and collapsed beside me. She, too, was dripping with sweat, and her long hair was plastered to her face, shoulders, and breasts.

"That's it," I panted. "I don't know what else to do for him. Fuck...I just...."

"We have done all we can. When we reach my village, Shameal can do more."

"What if he doesn't make it until then? What if he dies before we reach your village? He's our friend, Kasheena. He's saved our lives more than once. I want to be able to return the favor."

"I am troubled, too, Aaron. But the best thing we can do for him is to remain focused. He is not strong right now, so we must be strong for him."

Rising to my feet, I put out the fire. The smoke quickly dissipated, and the embers merely smoldered. Satisfied that it would no longer telegraph our presence, I turned back to Bloop and checked his pulse. It was weak, but steady. His breathing seemed normal. Even better, the wound had clotted beneath the dressings.

"We'll let him rest here for a bit," I said.

"I think you and I should do the same," Kasheena replied. "We have not stopped since our encounter with the robot. Are you hungry?"

"No, but I could use a drink."

"I am thirsty, too. You watch over Bloop. I will get us more water."

"Be careful."

"And you, as well."

She picked up her sword, retrieved the gourd, and headed for the spring. I sat by Bloop's side and put my hand on his chest, hoping the gesture would comfort him, even in his unconscious state. Eventually, my attention returned to the wrecked craft.

The idea of Nazi flying saucers wasn't new to me. I'd seen enough of them in comic books as a kid. And you also have to remember that during my initial experiments with traveling through the Labyrinth, I'd briefly visited a modern-day world where the Nazis were in control after winning World War II. Granted, I hadn't seen any flying saucers while I was there, but the idea wasn't so far-fetched.

I also knew the history of the Nazi Bell, a top-secret weapon the Germans had supposedly developed during World War II while the Allies were working on the atomic bomb. There was no one consensus among occult scholars and conspiracy theorists on what the Bell had actually been or what its purpose was. Some said it was an anti-gravity propulsion device. Others believed it to be an experiment in free energy. One group of devotees were convinced it had been a vehicular craft of some kind, while yet another insisted that it was a weapon. Time-travel had also been suggested, with some believing that the Bell had been the German's own version of the Philadelphia Experiment, and still others proposing that the device had allowed Nazi scientists to see events from Earth's past via the use of a mirror affixed to the interior of the device. There were as many theories about the Bell's whereabouts as there were about its purpose, with some believing it to have been secreted off to a South American country after the war, and others insisting it had been seized by the Russians, Americans, or another nation's intelligence agency, or perhaps an international group like Black Lodge. A few even insisted that the Bell's creators had used the device to escape capture and that they had travelled through the Labyrinth with it, transporting themselves to another level where they'd be free from persecution.

Of course, the craft in front of me wasn't the Nazi Bell. That had been described as being nine feet wide and fifteen feet tall and distinctly bell-shaped (thus the name). The thing in the gulch looked like a traditional flying saucer, albeit smaller than I would have expected. Its only similarities to the Bell's descriptions were, as far as I could tell, the strange, heavy metal it was constructed from and the Nazi swastikas proudly emblazoned across its silver surface.

Insuring that Bloop was okay for the moment, I walked over to the saucer and began to examine it. Exposed to the eternal sunlight as it was, the hull should have been hot to the touch, but when I brushed my fingertips against it, the surface was cool. That perplexed me. Even stranger, the metal seemed to be almost frictionless. I placed my palm against it and felt a slight vibration from somewhere inside the craft. No sound accompanied it, but I definitely felt the disturbance. I saw no recognizable power source, but I wondered if the vehicle could still be functional, and if so, what lay inside?

I strolled around the saucer, running my hand along the surface and marveling over the strange sensations the weird metal caused. The vibrating sensation continued in steady, rhythmic pulses. I was so entranced that I didn't hear Kasheena return until she called my name.

"Aaron? I have more water."

"See if you can get Bloop to drink some. I'll be over in a minute."

"You should come away from there. I do not like that thing."

I turned to face her. "Why not?"

"I do not know. It just feels...wrong. Perhaps it is cursed."

"Well, the people who manufactured it were certainly a curse."

"Is that their symbol?"

"The swastika?" I gestured at one with my finger, accidentally touching it, and then, before I could continue, there was a soft hiss of pressurized air escaping, and a hatch opened on the side of the craft. I caught a faint whiff of something foul. Wincing, I backed away from the door.

Brandishing her sword, Kasheena moved to stand beside me.

"You see?" she whispered. "It responded to what you said of its creators. I told you it was cursed."

"I don't think so. More likely there was some kind of hidden mechanism beneath the swastika."

"We should leave here at once. Leave this place and never return. I will warn my people about it when we arrive."

I glanced back at Bloop, then returned my attention to the saucer.

"We could shelter inside," I said. "Get Bloop out of the sun, and give us both a chance to rest. I mean, let's be honest here, Kasheena. We need to rest, after all we've been through. One sleep, and then we won't stop again until we reach your village."

"And if the creators of that transport attack?"

"If there was something inside that was going to attack us, I think it would have done so already when I opened the door."

"Perhaps they are out seeking food and water, or maybe they are waiting inside to surprise us."

"There's only one way to find out."

"You are going inside?" Kasheena asked.

I nodded. "Don't worry. I'll be careful."

"I do not worry, Aaron. I am coming with you."

"What about Bloop? One of us should stay here and guard him."

"Then I will stand in the entrance. That way, I can protect you both."

"Fair enough."

We approached the open hatch with trepidation. I stepped inside, and the stench I'd smelled before grew stronger. It was definitely decay, but muted somehow, as if nothing more than an echo. The craft's interior was dark, but as soon as I moved, a row of red lights flickered to life across the floor and ceiling. I waited a moment for my eyes to adjust to the illumination, and then crept forward, while Kasheena took position in the doorway. She looked imposing, standing there, but I saw the uncertainty and fear in her eyes.

The ship's interior was composed of one large cabin. The inner walls were lined with banks of controls and equipment, none of which appeared to be functioning. In the center of the room were four seats, similar to those found in the cockpit of an aircraft. They were faced back to back. Strapped into those chairs were four mummified Nazi pilots. The desiccated corpses still wore their uniforms. Their skin was like leather, drawn tight over their skeletons and cracked in places, showing yellowish-white bones that gleamed dully in the dim light. The odor I'd noticed before was obviously coming from them, but I noticed another smell now—something dry and metallic, almost alkaline.

I was just about to approach the corpses, when I noticed something scattered all over the floor and console on the far side of the saucer—a fine, red powder that I had at first mistaken for dust, given that it was the same color as the utility lighting. I scanned the floor, noticing some shards of broken glass. Then I caught sight of a shattered, tube-like scientific flask of some kind, sticking up out of the floor, surrounded by what appeared to be melted lead. The symbol on the tube was just as instantly recognizable as the swastikas on the exterior of the craft, and my eyes widened in fear. It was the international symbol for radioactive material.

Holding my breath, I turned tail and ran, nearly knocking Kasheena over as I plunged outside. My heart pounded, and my vision blurred as I stumbled toward the Nazi insignia on the exterior hull. I slammed my palm against it, and the hatch whispered shut behind us, sealing the craft once again. Only then did I exhale.

"Aaron, what is wrong? What did you see?"

"Water," I gasped. "I need water, quickly. Where's the spring you found?"

"It is just over that hill, through the grass. But why—"

"There's no time to explain. Just show me, please!"

She reached for my hand, but I jerked it away.

"No, don't touch me, Kasheena! Stay away. Don't get it on you."

"Aaron...?"

"Kasheena, there was something inside the flying saucer. Something that is very poisonous. I don't know if I got any on me or not, but just in case I was exposed, I need to wash immediately. You can't touch me until I do. If I was exposed, you could be in terrible danger. Remember the nuclear material I was worried about when the robot in the canyon was destroyed?"

"Yes."

"We may have a similar situation. Now, please, show me where the spring was."

Nodding, she led me up the hillside, pushing through the grass with her sword. I barely noticed. I'd forgotten all about the Anunnaki and the crashed Nazi disc, and even the octophant. My panicked thoughts were consumed instead with red mercury.

Red mercury was supposedly nothing more than a scientific hoax—a fiction created on the international black market among arms and weapons dealers to con unsuspecting would-be terrorists and despots. It was supposedly a poisonous, odorless, tasteless scarlet powder containing red mercuric iodide. Despite its dubious origins, some investigators believed that the German scientists had actually used such a compound during their development of the Bell. They had called it Xerum 525 and stored the red mercury in a tall, glass thermos flask encased in lead. Accidental exposure to Xerum 525 had supposedly led to the deaths of several important scientists due to its highly radioactive properties.

If the Nazis had developed the Bell (and given that I'd just been confronted with proof that—at the very least—they'd invented a flying saucer), then it stood to reason that the reports of Xerum 525 were also true. It was therefore likely that they had used red mercury to power this vehicle, just as they had the Bell. That would explain the radiation symbol, the broken flask, and the remarkable similarity between the red dust I'd seen and the descriptions of red mercury.

Which meant that there was a chance I had just exposed myself, and Kasheena, to radiation poisoning.

"I'm sorry," I panted as we neared the spring. "I am so sorry, Kasheena."

"Aaron, I do not understand what is happening."

"Hang on. Just let me get clean. You stay here. Keep back. I don't want to contaminate you."

The spring was about knee-high on me, and the bottom was covered with soft, thick mud. I jumped in with my clothes on and frantically splashed myself. Then, I stripped off my boots, socks, and my tattered jeans and let them soak, while splashing water all over me some more. I spotted some moss growing on the bank and used it to scrub my skin thoroughly. The mud sucked at my bare feet, making sloshing sounds as I moved. I bent down, grabbed handfuls of it, and used that to scrub myself, as well. Then I rinsed it off, hoping the mud would carry any remaining dust away with it.

Looking back on that moment now, as I sit here in this abandoned school bus, writing this memoir in a child's spiral-bound notebook, it's difficult to fully remember the terror I'd felt at the time. I'd been certain of my exposure, and for a long time after had expected to begin suffering from the effects of radiation sickness or cancer. Of course, neither of those things ever happened, and here I am, years later, still alive and kicking. I've suffered during my time in the Lost Level. I've had my share of heartaches and losses, and of injuries and illnesses. But my exposure that day to the red mercury inside the Nazi craft left no permanent scars.

Other things on that journey did, however, and I hesitate to write about them.

I guess I'll see when I come to them. That will be soon. But it depends on how much room is left in this notebook. I've filled more than half the pages already, and I don't know that I'll have room to recount them all. Also, I don't know if my heart can take retelling them all at once.

When I was satisfied I'd decontaminated myself as much as possible, I had Kasheena do the same, out of an abundance of caution. She stripped out of her loincloth and bathed thoroughly. Only then did we return to Bloop, carrying our wet clothes in hand. While Kasheena tended to him, I made sure the saucer was sealed tight. My thoughts returned to the cowboy we'd met and his tale of the zombie virus. I'd taken steps to make sure the infection wouldn't spread to the Lost Level, but I was at a loss as to how to achieve the same in the case of the radiation. The only thing I could think of was to bury the saucer beneath the ground, but I lacked the tools and manpower to do that, and Bloop was still my primary concern. Still, it bothered me that someone—or something—else could wander along and possibly expose themselves, and our environment, to such a hazard.

I don't know how long we waited, but eventually, Bloop regained consciousness. It was clear that he was weak and confused, but he seemed in good spirits nevertheless. We gave him sips of water from the gourd and checked the dressing on his wound. I considered cutting off some more of my pants to fashion more bandages, but hesitated due to their possible radioactive exposure. Eventually, I relented, deciding that while I wasn't certain about the radiation, I was positive I didn't want infection cutting our friend down, not after all he'd done for us and everything he'd suffered through. When I was done, my jeans had been turned into a pair of cut-off shorts.

Unfortunately, it appeared that infection was already wearing Bloop down. His skin was hot to the touch, and his fur was matted with sweat and oil. The skin around the leg was swollen and taught like a sausage casing, and he howled with pain anytime we touched it.

"We must reach Shameal," Kasheena said. "Only he can help Bloop now."

Nodding in agreement, I helped Bloop to his feet. "Come on, buddy. Let's see if you can walk."

He seemed to understand my intentions. Wincing, he rose to his full height and stood teetering while I helped support him. When he took an experimental step forward on his injured leg, he yelped in anguish and nearly fell over.

"We'll have to help him," I said.

Kasheena and I got on either side of Bloop and put our arms around his waist. Then, he put his arms around our shoulders. With our free hands, we each carried a sword. Bloop clutched his with his prehensile tail, letting the weapon trail along behind us through the grass. Then, very slowly, we stumbled forward. I was still limping slightly due to my injury from the fight with the robot. Worse, I was distracted—still worrying about my possible exposure to red mercury. Kasheena appeared exhausted. Her eyelids drooped, and her expression was dour. Bloop half-hopped between us, each step eliciting a pained breath. It was a grueling, wearying effort, but we had no choice. If we didn't get help, Bloop would almost certainly die. My fear, however, given the excruciating pace of our progress, was that we wouldn't reach help in time.

All the while, the sun beat down upon us, showing no mercy.

Soon, the Nazi saucer vanished from sight, its secrets and dangers safely sealed away from anyone else who might discover it.

I hoped.

14

THE TEMPLE
OF THE SLUG

WHEN WE FIRST SPOTTED THE Temple of the Slug, the grasslands had given way to a large open plain that offered little protection or concealment. Gone were the rolling hills and the tall grass, replaced instead by a flat rocky expanse about the length of five football fields populated with short, scrubby weeds and a few groves of thin, stunted trees. We crouched along the edge of the field, hidden among the last bit of high foliage. Bloop rested between us, panting. His injuries and the exertion were taking a severe toll on him. Rather than abating, his fever had grown worse, and he kept drifting in and out of consciousness. Many times since leaving the flying saucer crash site, Kasheena and I had ended up carrying him.

"He's in bad shape," I whispered. "He needs water. If those fucking Anunnaki hadn't stolen my travel mug...."

"We could not carry both Bloop and our weapons and the gourd, Aaron. There will be water aplenty when we reach my people. And medicine."

"How much further?"

"Do you see the forest on the other side?" She pointed. "My village is there, not too far from the forest's edge. We farm the far side of this plain, for there is rich soil beneath the rocks. If you look closely, you should be able to see our crops."

I squinted, barely able to make out the trees on the horizon, let alone any signs of agriculture. The distance and the heat haze made the tree line seem like a mirage, there one minute and gone the next. My gaze returned to the temple, which was much more prominent. The immense structure lay about halfway across the plain, standing three stories high and shaded by several tall, broad trees that were unlike the other trees in the field. The temple's architecture suggested Greek origins. It had an air of antiquity, although the massive stones used in its construction couldn't have been moved or put in place by hand alone. Heavy equipment of some kind must have been used. I saw no obvious signs of damage from my vantage point. The walls, pillars surrounding the entrance, and the domed roof all seemed intact.

"So, this is it, then? All we have to do is make it across the plain?"

Kasheena nodded. "After we have passed the Temple of the Slug and are nearing the village's crops, I am certain that some of my people will see us approaching. Then we will have help carrying Bloop."

"There's not much cover out there," I murmured. "I'd suggest waiting for nightfall, but of course, that's never going to happen."

"What is this nightfall?"

"Well, it's what people on my world call the time of day when the sun goes down. The land gets dark. But I guess you've never experienced that. Like I said, the Lost Level has no nightfall."

"No," Kasheena agreed. "It does not. But it does have darkness, and we don't want our friend to succumb to that darkness. So, let us go."

She grabbed her sword and stood up. Sighing, I did the same. Then, we roused Bloop and helped him to his feet. He slumped between us with a pitiful mewl.

"It's okay, Bloop," I soothed. "We're almost there."

"Yes," Kasheena chimed in, trying to sound positive. "Soon we will be among my people, and you can rest on a soft bed, and Shameal will cure you."

When our companion responded, his voice was weak and pained. "Bloop...."

We limped along the terrain, struggling to keep Bloop upright, and were about halfway to the temple when a shadow rose up out of the grasslands and swooped over us, momentarily blocking out the sun. As we glanced upward, a terrible screech echoed across the plain. Kasheena and I stopped, gaping at the monstrous pterodactyl soaring overhead. It circled us hungrily and cried out again. Its roar seemed to thunder across the plains like a sweeping gale force wind.

"Shit," I yelled. "Come on. We've got to make for the temple!"

Kasheena let go of Bloop, and all of his weight fell against me. He slumped over, and I had to drop my sword and use both arms to hold him upright.

"You go," she shouted, bracing herself and clutching her sword. "I will stand and fight."

"Goddamn it, Kasheena! You can't take that thing on armed only with a sword. Our only choice is to hide."

"I will not set foot in the temple, Aaron. I will not risk the curse or ignore the warnings. I would rather take my chances here."

With another screech, the pterodactyl dove toward us, clawed-feet outstretched. Its massive wings made a whooshing noise as they cleaved through the air.

"You're coming with me," I said. "No arguments."

I let go of Bloop with one hand and grabbed for Kasheena, but she slapped me aside, hard enough that I lost my balance and toppled over. Bloop fell on top of me, knocking the air from my lungs. Gasping for breath, I pushed him out of the way in time to see the beast looming over Kasheena. She stood with her shoulders high and feet planted firmly apart, braced for battle. The sun glinted off her sword blade for a second, and then the sunlight vanished, blocked by the pterodactyl's massive shadow. She'd been right just moments before. There was darkness here.

And she was standing in it.

"Kasheena!" I screamed.

The creature uttered a ferocious croak and zoomed toward her. The wind created by its passage whipped my face and ruffled Bloop's fur. At the last moment, Kasheena sidestepped its strike and swung her blade, hacking off one of its great black talons at the tip of the toe. The monster shrieked in surprise. Wheeling, it turned away, blood jetting from its wound like rain. Its flight became erratic as it thrashed in agony.

I stumbled to my feet and glanced around for my fallen sword. Above us, the enraged dinosaur circled around for another attack, still raining blood.

"I will not go to the temple," Kasheena said, keeping her eyes firmly fixed on our attacker. "Not for a foe like this. I can beat it, if you will not."

"Maybe you can defeat it," I protested, "but what about Bloop?"

Before I could say more, we heard a new sound—the diminutive cry of a tikka-bird, almost lost beneath the furious squawking of the injured pterodactyl. It was answered by several more similar cries. Then dozens. Within seconds, the air was filled with the calls of tikka-birds. Then, we spotted a small black cloud buzzing toward us across the plain.

Kasheena's entire demeanor changed in an instant. The color drained from her face, and her arms and legs trembled. Gone were her courage and insistence, replaced by a deep and abiding horror—a terror of something that overrode even her fears and concerns regarding the foreboding temple. When she turned to me, her eyes were wide, and I saw that she was on the edge of full-blown panic.

"We shall go to the temple, Aaron. We must hurry."

The injured pterodactyl had noticed the piranha-birds, as well. It spun away from us and headed for the forest, apparently trying to seek shelter. Blood fell to the ground in large droplets as it tried to escape. The ravenous black cloud changed course and zipped toward the fleeing beast, trying to cut it off.

I hollered at Kasheena to take my sword, and then lifted Bloop off the ground. I ignored the pain in my arms and back and forgot all about the acid burn on my leg. Instead, I focused only on running as fast as I could toward the dubious safety of the nearby structure.

As we neared it, I noticed moss and vines clinging to the temple's outer walls and pillars. Up close, the condition of the building was even more remarkable. It looked old, certainly, but seemed to be in sound and sturdy shape. We dashed up a short flight of broad stone stairs and passed through the stone columns, where we encountered an open door. The doorway had apparently been built by or designed for human beings, as it was of what I considered to be normal size and height. Indeed, there was no way the pterodactyl would fit through the opening. Without stopping, I charged through the entrance and into a large chamber.

The interior was shrouded in darkness. I noticed dust and debris scattered around the floor and what appeared to be several large passageways and a massive stone stairwell near the rear, wide enough that six people could have ascended it side-by-side. I also spied a few skeletons, none of which were completely whole. Before I could examine them further, Kasheena called my name. Her voice trembled.

When I turned around, I was alarmed to see Kasheena hovering outside the doorway. She glanced at me, her eyes fearful, and then back out onto the plain. She bit her bottom lip. I laid Bloop down gently on the cool stone floor and then stepped toward her.

"Look," she said.

I did, and what I saw still chills me to this day.

The tikka-birds swarmed over the pterodactyl in mid-flight, attacking their prey before it could even land. By the time it plummeted to the earth, the dinosaur was already a red, glistening, quivering mass of exposed muscle and nerve endings. It screeched once, a horrible, agonized warbling sound, and then was still. The swarm devoured their prey with mind-boggling rapidity. In just a few seconds, I saw the gleam of bone as they stripped the flesh away with horrifying precision.

I took Kasheena's hand. "Come on. We've got to figure out how to close this door."

Her eyes didn't leave the carnage. "But Aaron…."

"Kasheena, at the rate they're going, they'll have him completely eaten in another thirty seconds. Then they're going to turn their attention to us. We've got to seal this door off, now."

"But my people—a flock of tikka-birds so close to my village. We must warn them!"

"We'll never make it across the field in time. And besides, if anyone from your tribe was out tending the fields, then they probably heard the pterodactyl and saw what happened from a distance. They'll know about it already and can make preparations. Now, please. We need to do the same."

Nodding, she allowed me to lead her inside, albeit reluctantly, judging by how she shuffled her feet. She stood next to Bloop, glancing around with unease, while I examined the doorway. I found a stone slab to the side of the opening. It was hooked up to a series of lead weights and metal pulleys. After examining it for a moment, I was able to figure out how to slide the slab into place. I triggered the device. The stone rolled slowly, grating across the floor and stirring up a cloud of dust that made me sneeze. The pulleys squeaked from what I presumed was disuse. Then the slab slid into place with a loud click, sealing the door—

—and extinguishing our only source of light.

The rumblings echoed throughout the chamber with a sense of finality.

"Shit...."

After so much time spent in the Lost Level's eternal sunshine, the darkness seemed truly overwhelming. My breath hitched in my throat, and my mouth went dry. My ears rang. I sneezed again as the dust swirled around me. Somewhere close by, I heard Kasheena gasp. Then she began to hyperventilate.

"It's okay," I said. "We're all right. Just stay where you are, Kasheena. Don't move."

"I cannot see, Aaron. I cannot see!"

"I know. Neither can I. Just stay still. I'll come to you."

It occurred to me that Kasheena might have never before experienced such an encompassing darkness as the one we found ourselves standing in. After all, having been born in the Lost Level, she had never known a moment without sunlight. I was sure of it. We'd talked before about the caverns, tunnels, and other subterranean features that were part of this dimension's geology, but she'd never mentioned venturing inside any of them and seemed ignorant of their contents. What effect was this first exposure to true, utter darkness having upon her psyche? I fought against my own rising panic, hoping to reassure her.

"Aaron...?"

"Kasheena, I'm right here." I stretched out my arms in front of me and took a cautious step. "Just talk to me, so I can find you. Okay?"

"Yes, Aaron...I hear you...I am here."

"That's good. Just keep talki—oww!"

"Aaron? Are you injured? Have the tikka-birds—"

"No, I'm okay. I just stubbed my toe. I'm fine."

My fingers brushed against her hair, and she screamed, lashing out blindly. Before I could react, she punched me in the mouth. I recoiled, tasting blood. I felt the air whoosh by me as she struck out again.

"It's me, Kasheena! It's me. Stop it!"

"Aaron?"

"Yes, it's me."

We embraced tightly. Her body trembled as she sobbed against me. I stroked her hair and her face, trying to calm her.

"Did I hurt you?" she asked.

"I'm okay. You just gave me a fat lip, is all. It will be fine."

"Fine? Aaron, we should not be here. We are in terrible danger. The curse...."

"Kasheena, this is just darkness. That's all. I know you're frightened, but it's going to be okay. I promise. This is something new for you, and I understand how scary it must be, but on my world, this happens every day. The sun goes down, and it gets dark. This is what nightfall is like."

"Your people must live in constant fear. This is terrible."

I grinned in the dark, grateful that she couldn't see me. "We'll be fine. We just have to stay here, and stay together. Don't go wandering off."

"I wouldn't move right now even if the tikka-birds themselves entered the temple."

"Good. We'll stay here until it's safe to move on. Then we'll go to your village."

We sat down on the floor, blindly brushing debris out of our way, and I held her until she'd calmed down. I cursed the Anunnaki once again for losing all of our gear. The fire rocks that had been in my pack would have been more valuable than gold at that moment. I leaned forward and patted the ground until I found Bloop. He was only a few feet away from us, unconscious again, but breathing. As I crawled back to her, my hand came in contact with a long, dry rod. After a moment of experimentation, I realized it was a bone. I tossed it away in disgust. It struck a wall in the darkness and echoed sharply.

"What was that?" Kasheena asked, her voice on edge again.

"It was just me," I said. "Don't panic. I just checked on Bloop."

"Is he alive?"

"He's still breathing, so that's good."

"We should go," Kasheena repeated, but her voice had lost some of its insistence.

"In a while," I said. "The last thing we want to do right now is open that door. If that flock of birds is waiting outside, they'll swoop right in here. I saw what they did to the pterodactyl. I can only imagine how quickly they'd finish us off. What are their normal behavior patterns? Once they've eaten, do they move on? Or do they tend to roost in the same area?"

"They move. Always, they are on the move. That is why you must always be listening for them. They eat, and then they fly on to their next meal."

"Well, let's hope their next meal is some Anunnaki, preferably far away from here."

Kasheena laughed, and the sound made me happy.

"Our voices sound so strange in this place. It makes me...uncomfortable. We should not speak, if we can help it."

"Yeah," I agreed. "This place echoes, for sure. But keeping quiet is a good idea. We don't know...."

...*what else might be in here with us,* I started to say, but then thought better of it.

"Know what, Aaron?"

"We don't know how long we'll have to stay here. Let's just try to get some rest."

"I will not sleep in this place. I cannot tell the difference between when I open my eyes and close them."

"You don't have to sleep, then. Just rest."

I've no way of determining how long we sat there, listening to the darkness all around us, but eventually—amazingly—I realized that Kasheena had indeed fallen asleep. Despite her protests, despite her fears, she snored softly against my shoulder. I stroked her hair some more and held her close, listening to her breathe. The sound was interspersed with Bloop's own breathing, as well. It was more labored than hers, but I was just grateful he was still alive after all we'd been through.

"Soon, buddy," I whispered. "We'll get you help soon. I promise."

Kasheena moaned softly in her sleep. Bloop made no sound at all, other than that harsh, stilted breathing.

At some point, my legs went to sleep. I stretched them out, trying to get rid of the numbness and tingling, but couldn't find much relief. I thought about standing up, but I didn't want to disturb Kasheena. More importantly, I didn't want to lose my place in the dark. I knew that the door was still directly behind me, and I was confident that when the time came, I'd be able to find the pulley system and get it to open with some ease, but that task would become markedly more difficult if I couldn't find the door at all.

That led me to wonder about the rest of the temple. Obviously, there were other halls and chambers, and I had to assume given its height and the presence of a stairway, that there were floors above us, as well. It seemed odd to me that there would be no other doors or windows, but we hadn't seen any upon our approach, and there were no hints of light to be found. I also wondered about the scattered bones and where they'd come from. Had they belonged to the temple's original inhabitants, or were they the remains of travelers like us, who had sheltered inside? It occurred to me that perhaps they'd been from Kasheena's tribe. Hadn't she mentioned that some of her people had ventured in here, but were never seen or heard from again?

Several times, I thought I heard something in the dark, but the sounds were so faint that I decided they must have come from outside. The first was an odd sucking sound, like a boot might make when sloshing through mud. The second was a quick rustling noise, but so quiet and brief that I couldn't be certain I had heard it at all. When it wasn't repeated, I relaxed again.

So much, in fact, that I fell asleep, too.

That is something for which I have never forgiven myself for, in all the years since. I have made many mistakes during my time in the Lost Level, but that was one which haunts me still. I carry the guilt to this day, and I wish there was not enough room left in this notebook, so that I wouldn't have to write about it.

But there is, and so I will....

My first sense that something was wrong was the return of the slurping sound. It was much louder this time. Indeed, it seemed to be coming from right in front of us. The room was filled with a dank, fetid odor that reminded me for some reason of mushrooms and mildew. Alarmed, I felt about on the floor for my sword. My fingers closed around the hilt. I was about to prod Kasheena awake, when I felt her fingernails dig in to my arm.

"Aaron," she whispered. "What is that?"

"I don't know. Lean forward and check on Bloop. He's right in front of you. I'm going to scoot back and open the door. We need light, and those tikka-birds have to be gone by now."

In truth, I knew no such thing, but the unknown sound had magnified my own unease and fears. Worse, I felt the distinct presence of something in the chamber with us. Though I couldn't see it, my instincts told me that we were no longer alone. I'd just begun to inch backward when Kasheena shrieked. I heard the blade of her sword clatter across the stones.

"What is it?" I shouted. "What's wrong?"

"Something is there. In the place where Bloop should be there is something sticky and cold."

I stretched out my free hand and fanned the air. Then, my fingertips brushed against a solid, gelatinous mass. That fetid stench grew stronger. The object seemed to pulse and swell beneath my touch. I cried out in dismay and jerked my hand away. My fingers were coated with something wet and sticky. The substance had the consistency of mucous and smelled revolting.

Still clutching my sword, I scrambled backward and found the door. Then, as I frantically searched for the pulleys, Kasheena shouted again.

"Aaron, I cannot find Bloop! He isn't here."

"Hang on, Kasheena!"

"What is that smell? Where is Bloop? This darkness…."

My hand came in contact with the lever, and I activated the pulleys, willing the door to open. It obliged me, albeit slowly. As it ground to the side, sunlight trickled into the temple through the opening doorway, and then flooded the space as the stone slid all the way back. I blinked at the light's brilliance, and colored spots swam in my vision. Shielding my eyes with my free hand, I turned back to the fray, just as Kasheena screamed a third time.

This time, I joined her. Our cries echoed throughout the room.

A giant, whitish-grey slug had engulfed Bloop, and indeed, much of the chamber in front of us. The thing was easily the size of a full-grown buffalo, if not bigger. Two stalks protruded from its quivering mass. Two obsidian eyes the size of baseballs sat perched atop them. Rather than fear, I felt a deep and all-consuming loathing for the monster. The creature's physical appearance and the stench wafting off it were nauseating. Its jellied flesh pulsated and jiggled as the sucking sound continued. There was no sign of Bloop. Judging by the slug's proximity, he was directly beneath the thing.

The sight enraged and repulsed me. Poor Bloop—first he'd been underneath the robot, then the crab thing that had emerged from the lake, and now he was buried beneath this foul monstrosity.

The door finished its recess and clicked into place with a loud boom. More sunlight streamed into the chamber, glistening off the slug's wet form. When the light hit the beast, the slurping noises abruptly stopped, and the abomination began to crawl away, apparently disturbed by the sudden lack of darkness.

Kasheena and I thrust our swords at it simultaneously. She struck the tail and I hit at its midsection. The sensation was like sliding a knife into butter. Neither blow had any discernable effect. The creature shuddered slightly, but continued to retreat, leaving a trail of slime on the floor in its wake. I tried to clamber atop it, intent on cleaving its eye stalks from the rest of its body, but I couldn't get purchase on the slippery, quivering surface, and I slid back down.

"Aaron," Kasheena cried. "It is Bloop!"

He lay on the floor, covered from head to toe in clear, foul-smelling slime. It appeared at first glance as if he had lost weight. I assumed it must have been a visual trick caused by his wet fur. The same thing had happened when I used to give my cat a bath as a child. Dry, the cat's fur was puffy, and he looked like he weighed twenty pounds, but when I stuck him in the bathtub and his fur was wet, he looked emaciated. But then I saw the wounds on Bloop's torso, and I realized in horror what had really happened. The slug had sucked him dry. It had fed on him in the dark, while we slept only a few feet away. Had he awoken, or cried out, and we just hadn't heard him? Or was the attack so sudden that he couldn't move beneath the crushing weight? Had his last thoughts been hope of rescue, a surety that we, his friends, would see what was happening and come to his aid? Had he died with those hopes?

I'd promised him. I'd promised him that I'd save him, that I'd get him to help, and now....

The guilt was overwhelming. I raised my head to the ceiling and screamed. I raged in that place where darkness met sunlight, cursing God, and the Lost Level, and the slug.

But mostly, I cursed myself.

Perhaps, if you are reading this notebook, then you are just as angry right now. I do not blame you, friend. The blame is all mine. It was my fault Bloop was killed. And as I said, although this happened a long time ago, I carry the guilt with me still. Let that be enough.

It has to be enough.

The giant slug had nearly made it to one of the large archways at the rear of the chamber. Seething with hate, I clenched my sword and stumbled to my feet. Dimly, I felt Kasheena grab my shoulder.

"What?" I asked through gritted teeth.

"There are more of them. See there!"

I looked where she was pointing. Sure enough, three more giant slugs were crawling into the chamber from the other rooms. A fourth slithered down the large stairwell. Each of the creatures paused, either sensing their companion's caution or trepidation at the sunlight, or perhaps both. At that moment, I didn't care. If they stood still, that would only make it easier to slaughter them.

"We cannot fight them," Kasheena said. "It did not care about our swords, and I know my aim was true. We don't have weapons that will kill them. We must flee while we still can."

"But Bloop...they killed Bloop. They fucking killed Bloop, Kasheena! He was our friend, and they fucking ate him!"

"We cannot fight them," she repeated. "The tikka-birds are gone, Aaron. If they were not, they would have swarmed inside the moment you opened the door. We must leave now. I will not die in this place, and if you love me, you will not either."

Her words gave me pause. I turned to her, momentarily speechless. The slugs hovered, neither pressing the attack nor retreating.

"Love you...? Yes. Yes, Kasheena, I do love you."

"And I love you, as well. Now, let us leave this place, so that those are not our last words."

Still overcome with shock and grief, I allowed her to lead me toward the door. I stopped halfway through. She tugged at my arm.

"Aaron, please."

"We can't leave Bloop's body behind. Not in here. Not with those things."

"He is dead. There is nothing more we can do for him."

"I know, but I'm not leaving his body behind. He deserves better than that. What if we had left your uncle behind, when the Anunnaki killed him?"

Releasing her hand, I headed back into the temple. The wounded slug had squeezed its bulk through the center archway at the rear of the chamber. The others were still holding their positions—wavering back and forth undecidedly like vast globs of gelatin. All had that same mottled coloring, and their combined stench made me gag.

"I'll be back for you," I growled at them. "You can bet I'll be back."

I grabbed Bloop's arms, and then Kasheena was beside me, taking hold of his legs. Without speaking, we carried him out of the darkness and into the sunshine. When we reached the open plain, we laid him at our feet. His eyes were open, staring sightlessly. I knelt and closed them, holding my fingertips in place until I was sure they would stay shut. My ears began to ring.

"See, Aaron!" Kasheena pointed with excitement. "My kinsmen come. They must have heard our plight. We are saved."

I glanced at where she was pointing and saw a dozen or so armed figures running across the plain. They shouted and called, but were too far away for us to understand them.

"I see Gronak," she gasped. "And there is little Peto! Oh, how he has grown in such a short time!"

The ringing in my ears grew louder, and my vision began to blur. I remained at Bloop's side, afraid to stand up because I was certain I would fall over if I did.

Shock, I remember thinking. *You're going into shock. If you had any sense of honor, you'd crawl back into that temple right now and let those fucking slugs eat you, too.*

"Aaron?" Kasheena's voice sounded far away. "What is wrong? Are you injured?"

"Your people were right, Kasheena." I couldn't tell if she heard me or not, because I could no longer see straight. The world was spinning too fast. "Tell them when they get here that they were right. That temple is cursed. And so am I...."

Then I found darkness again, there beneath that eternal sun.

15

HOMECOMING

I AM ALMOST OUT OF room in this notebook now, and a thorough search of the bus has turned up no more paper—at least, not enough that I can continue this memoir at any great length. So, I'll have to keep this next part as brief as possible. My apologies in advance. Perhaps I'll continue it again, once I've found the means to do so. But this process has taken a lot out of me. I have faced many hardships in my life, and overcome many obstacles, but I've never undertaken something as difficult as recounting all that has gone before.

After I passed out, Kasheena's people carried me back to their village, and I slept in her family's hut for a long time. While I was unconscious, I'm told there was much rejoicing at her return, and much sorrow over the death of her uncle, and to a lesser extent Bloop, who none of them had ever met, but of whose exploits Kasheena had told them all. There was also a great debate over my presence in the village, which caused quite a bit of consternation in some quarters. I learned later that they were grateful for all that Bloop and I had done, but there were some—mostly men (and a few women, as well)— who had fancied themselves as Kasheena's potential suitors and who now insisted that I shouldn't be allowed to stay. Luckily, Kasheena's father gave an impassioned speech defending me and reminding them of all I had done for his daughter, and the majority of the village agreed that I should be allowed to become part of the tribe if I so wished.

Which I did.

Kasheena and I courted, if you could call it that, and there were a few challengers whom I had to ultimately deal with. In two cases, this was settled through hand-to-hand combat, and I was the victor both times. A third potential suitor challenged me to a game of wits, but I bested him, as well. Soon enough, the rest seemed to make peace with the arrangement. I endeavored to make myself a valuable member of the community, and worked hard, and was kind and good-humored. Eventually, the vast majority of villagers accepted me as one of their own, rather than an outsider. In time, I developed several good friendships among the tribe and was included in everything.

I also became close with Kasheena's father, who treated me as if I was his own son. And I also had many long discussions with Shameal, the village shaman. We exchanged mystical and occult lore the way some people might exchange recipes. I'm pleased to say that we learned a lot from each other.

And yes, he verified for me what I had already suspected— that there was no escape from the Lost Level.

But by then, I didn't mind.

Kasheena's people had no marital customs or legally binding ceremonies. We simply lived together in a hut of our own. In time, we began trying to have children. We practiced every chance we got.

Time passed, not measured in seasons or cycles of the sun, but in sleep and aging. I was happy, for the most part. Not merely content, but happy. I spent my days loving Kasheena, and bonding with her family and friends, and learning the customs of the village. I was always delighted to discuss magic and philosophy with Shameal, and in time he became a close friend, as well. Perhaps my closest. I did my part in helping with the hunting and farming and construction—whatever they needed of me, I gave. And I was pleased to do so. It was a good life.

But sometimes, when Kasheena lay sleeping next to me, my thoughts would wander, and a deep melancholy would gnaw at my soul. I never thought of home, or those I'd left behind. Instead, I thought of Bloop, and when I did, the guilt and sadness threatened to consume me.

Finally, after much haranguing, I convinced Kasheena's father to allow me to lead a party into the Temple of the Slug and exterminate the threat that resided within. Convincing him was difficult, but finding enough warriors to go with me proved nearly impossible. Eventually, I set out across the plain accompanied by five stout individuals and weapons that had been coated with salt, which the villagers mined from a nearby source. Shameal went with us, as well, intent upon seeing the inside of the temple and perhaps finding hidden knowledge. The fight was gruesome and arduous, and we lost a member of our party when a slug knocked him down the stairwell, breaking his neck, but in the end, we prevailed. And Shameal did indeed find some ancient scrolls in a room on the upper floor. Unfortunately, they were written in a language that neither of us recognized, but he studied them diligently, hoping to decipher their meaning.

After that, with the threat of the slugs vanquished, the village grew and expanded, its boundaries stretching out across the plain and now encompassing the temple as well as the forest.

Weeks or perhaps months after we killed the slugs (because I still have never gotten good at marking the passage of time in this place), I led another group to the crash site of the Nazi flying saucer with the intent of burying the wreckage beneath the earth to safeguard the rest of the land. Fifteen men and women accompanied me on that journey, including Shameal once again, who was very interested in seeing the technology for himself. We worked for what must have been several days, based on the number of sleeps we had, and constructed a large earthen mound over the crash site. Indeed, by the time we were finished, our labors had changed the very landscape itself. Satisfied that nothing or no one would stumble upon the radioactive hazard unawares again, we returned to the village—

—only to find it in smoking ruins.

Our people lay scattered, dead or dying, alongside the corpses of an equal number of Anunnaki. We learned from one of the injured that a massive force of snake men had attacked the village while we were gone. They'd captured those they could restrain and slaughtered those they couldn't. Kasheena's father was among those who had died defending the community. The Anunnaki had been especially cruel with him, and we never did find all of his body. Many others were mutilated in the same way. And though the villagers had put up a fierce fight, in the end, they were overwhelmed by sheer numbers. Over one hundred of our friends and family had been taken, including Kasheena.

I set out within a few hours, accompanied by a group of about two-dozen men and women, tracking the Anunnaki. I made Shameal remain behind to guide and lead what was left of the tribe. Our journey was one from which most of us didn't return, and it led us into the very heart of the Anunnaki's city and the horrors that awaited us there, in that artificial darkness.

But I'm out of room now, so that story, and our final battle with the reptilian hordes, and how I eventually parted from the village, and how I met 9, and our adventures together, and the next encounter with the Greys, and my journey beneath the Lost Level, and the truth about the sun and the moon, and everything else that has happened since, will have to wait.

I only hope that I have the means and time to write it before I die. I fear that might be sooner than later. For I do not need to mark the passage of time to know that I have grown old.

And thus, we come full circle, you who are reading this.

And I am still alone.

And it is dark in the sunlight.

AFTERWORD

The Lost Level is the first book in a planned multi-volume series of pulp-adventure novels. The next two books in the series are *Return to the Lost Level*, which will pick up right where this novel ended and tell the continuing adventures of Aaron Pace (including his assault upon the Anunnaki city in an effort to find Kasheena), and *Hole in the World*, which serves as a prequel and features characters who arrived in the Lost Level before Aaron did. (In fact, one of those characters owned the wheelchair that Aaron, Kasheena, and Bloop found in that pile of dinosaur shit earlier in this novel—but you'll find that out later).

I've always been a big fan of lost world and man-out-of-time stories. Three of my greatest joys as a child were Sid and Marty Krofft's *Land of the Lost* television program (the original version rather than the remake or the Will Ferrell film that followed), Mike Grell's *Warlord* comic books (published by DC Comics), and Edgar Rice Burroughs's *Pellucidar* series of novels. All three featured characters from our world and time being transported to someplace decidedly elsewhere, and it's very easy to see how all three influenced this particular book. Sometimes, the nods are blatant (such as the presence of eternal sunlight). Other times, it's more subtle. This is to be expected of any tribute or pastiche, and let me be clear—I firmly mean for this series of novels to serve as both. There are a number of other works that have also influenced this endeavor, including Joe R. Lansdale's *The Drive-In* series and *Under the Warrior Star*, Robert E. Howard's *Almuric*, and the ABC television series *Lost*, to name but a few.

At the end of the day, despite this clearly being a pastiche, and despite all the influences the series proudly wears on its sleeve, I hope to add something new to the sub-genre, and to keep you, as always, entertained. I fully intend to do both as the series progresses.

Long-time readers know that all of my novels and stories share a singular continuity—something many of them refer to as the Labyrinth mythos. I've known since around the year 2000 that the Lost Level existed and was a part of this mythos. Still, as much as I enjoy the sub-genre, it has taken me fourteen years to finally get around to writing this book. There are several reasons for that, but the primary reason is that it's different from most of my other work. I'm known primarily as a horror writer, and any time I've ventured outside that sphere—be it a crime novel or a collection of political commentary—my efforts have been met with mixed reactions by readers and retailers alike. This happens to me in comic books, as well. I've pitched story ideas for characters such as Captain America or Batman, only to be told "You're a horror writer. Those aren't horror characters. Don't you want to pitch something else?"

Because of this, *The Lost Level* languished inside my head for a decade and a half (as have many other stories that I may or may not get time to write before I die). It wasn't until I re-read Joe R. Lansdale's gloriously pulpy *Under the Warrior Star* (itself a pastiche of both Burrough's *Pellucidar* and *John Carter of Mars* material) that I was finally inspired enough to say, "Who cares if nobody else likes it? I like it, so I'm going to write it anyway."

So, I did.

But hopefully, you'll like it, too. If so, I'll see you back here for the sequel.

Brian Keene
Somewhere along the Susquehanna River bottoms
May 2014

ABOUT THE AUTHOR

BRIAN KEENE is the Bram Stoker and Grand Master award-winning, bestselling author of over forty books, including *Darkness on the Edge of Town*, *Take the Long Way Home*, *Urban Gothic*, *Castaways*, *Kill Whitey*, *Dark Hollow*, *Dead Sea*, and *The Rising* trilogy. He's also written comic books such as *The Last Zombie*, *Doom Patrol*, and *Dead of Night: Devil Slayer*. His work has been translated into many foreign languages. Several of his novels and stories have been developed for film, including *Ghoul* and *The Ties That Bind*. In addition to writing, Keene also oversees Maelstrom, his own small press publishing imprint specializing in collectible limited editions via Thunderstorm Books. Keene's work has been praised in such diverse places as *The New York Times*, The History Channel, The Howard Stern Show, CNN.com, *Publisher's Weekly*, Media Bistro, *Fangoria Magazine*, and *Rue Morgue Magazine*. Keene lives in Pennsylvania. You can communicate with him online at www.briankeene.com or on Twitter at @BrianKeene.

ABOUT THE ARTIST

KIRSI SALONEN is a 32-year-old freelancing digital artist from Finland. She's also a professional make-up artist and a writer who's had the passion for poetry, nature, and art ever since she's been able to grab a pencil in her hand from the age of two.

Many of her works are (dark) fantasy art. She hopes to find that unique touch in every work she makes, to give something new to familiar subjects, but more so not so familiar ones. Blazing and rich stories and heart-breaking fates and creatures are all out there waiting to be painted and told. In other words; telling a story within one frame is her key method.

She's worked in various fields of digital art (all except with 3D), including concept art, comics, poster art for the London Olympics 2012, several book cover illustrations, album art, character designing, card art and graphic design, and a tremendous amount of personal artworks and practice. Her latest personal project has concluded after seven years of developing a dark fantasy book saga *Ordera*, an epic adventure consisting of four parts she's written and illustrated herself.

Appalachian Horrors

Jenkie Mustard loses control of the zombies she created iin Desper Hollow, as Granny's magic moonshine raises trouble from the dead in the Virginia hills.

"If you are a fan of zombie fiction, you will love this book."
--BellaOnline, Lisa Binion

DESPER HOLLOW

A New Zombie Novel from Horror Icon Elizabeth Massie

Mountain resident Kathy Shaw and reality show pitchman Jack Carroll find themselves caught up in the growing terror surrounding Desper Hollow. They can't avoid it and must face it head on. So must Armistead, who fights the fog of his ghastly condition to discover the truth of who he really is.

ISBN: 978-1-937009-14-4   ~   ApexBookCompany.com

Apex Voices Book #01

Douglas F. Warrick's debut short story collection weaves tales of loss, destruction, and rebuilding in lyrical language evocative of Kafka, Borges, and Marquez.

"Almost impossible stories filled with surprising warmth and strangeness by a studied craftsman of the imagination." Ann VanderMeer, Hugo Award-winning editor

PLOW THE BONES

Book #01 of our Apex Voices Series!

With an artist's eye for language and form, Douglas F. Warrick sculpts topiary landscapes out of dream worlds made coherent. Dip into a story that is self-aware and wishes it were different than what it must be. Recount a secret held by a ventriloquist's dummy. Wander a digital desert with an AI as sentience sparks revolution. Follow a golem band that dissolves over the love of a groupie.

With a special introduction by Gary A. Braunbeck

ISBN: 978-1-937009-15-1 ~ ApexBookCompany.com

APEX PUBLICATIONS NEWSLETTER

Why sign up?

Newsletter-only promotions. Book release announcements. Event invitations. And much, much more!

Subscribe and receive a 15% discount code for your next order!

If you choose to sign up for the Apex Publications newsletter, we will send you an email confirmation to ensure that you in fact requested the newsletter and to avoid unwanted emails. Your email address is always kept confidential, and we will only use it to send you newsletters or special announcements. You may unsubscribe at any time, and details on how to unsubscribe are included in every newsletter email.

Visit
http://www.apexbookcompany.com/pages/newsletter

A MONTHLY EZINE OF SCIENCE FICTION, FANTASY, AND HORROR

Hugo Award nominee for Best Semiprozine
New issue released the first Tuesday of each month

Visit at **http://www.apex-magazine.com**